A DIXIE MORRIS ANIMAL ADVENTURE

DIXIE & CHAMP

GILBERT MORRIS

D1264127

MOODY PRESS
CHICAGO

To Miss Evelyn—
a good friend and
spiritual leader
Love,
Dixie

CONTENTS

1
ENCOUNTER IN THE WOODS

Whenever Dixie had school trouble, it was always in Mrs. McGeltner's class. This was strange because actually Dixie liked English and she liked most of her teachers.

Mrs. McGeltner, however, had a personality that grated on Dixie. She was a short, heavyset woman with steel gray hair and eyes. She also wanted her students to hand in perfect papers. Since most of them never did, this kept Mrs. McGeltner in a state of irritation.

Today Mrs. McGeltner had lived up to her reputation from the time class started. She had snapped at three students for not saying "Here" loudly enough when she called the roll.

When she wrote on the chalkboard,

"Assignment for Wednesday. Write a paper on the subject of American government," a groan went up.

Billy Joe Satterfield, who should have known better, said loudly, "But this is English class!"

"Class," Mrs. McGeltner barked, "a writer should be able to write on a variety of subjects!"

Billy Joe nodded. "I want to write on how I won the baseball game last week." Billy Joe was a big twelve-year-old with a thatch of blazing red hair.

"I don't want to hear any more stories of how you won the championship, Billy Joe," Mrs. McGeltner said firmly. "Now, this paper is to be three pages long . . ."

Another groan filled the classroom.

"Three pages!" Ollie Peck gasped.

"That is for Wednesday. Today, as you know, I'm going to give you half the class period to write a poem. This time you *can* write about anything you like. The only thing you must do is to write about how you *feel* about whatever it is you write about."

"That'll be easy." Billy Joe was talking again. "Do we get extra points for extragood poems?"

Francine Mosely, sitting in front of Billy Joe, gave him a withering look. "I don't think you're going to win any prizes," she whispered.

Francine had auburn hair and brown eyes and wore expensive clothing. Her father owned lots of timber and livestock. Francine nodded as if to say, "The rest of you can try, but *I* am going to write the best poem."

For the next twenty minutes most of the class worked on their poems. A few students scribbled something, then stared out the window.

But Dixie liked to write poetry. She stopped only twice to glance at Francine, sitting across from her. If she disliked any girl in school, this would be the one! Francine never missed a chance to let Dixie know what she thought of her taste in clothes and everything else.

Each time Dixie looked at her, Francine gave a satisfied smirk as if to say, "Who do you think you are, competing with *me?*"

Then Mrs. McGeltner said, "All right, time's up!"

A sigh of relief went up from some, but Dixie was pleased with her poem. It was one of the best she had ever written, she thought.

"Who would like to read your poem to the class?"

Only two hands shot up, Dixie's and Francine's.

"All right, Francine. You may read yours."

Francine stood and read her poem in a loud, clear voice, as if on a stage:

> "The wind is nice.
>   And so is ice.
>   When the wind blows
>   It's going to snow.
>
> "Every day in the sky
>   The clouds are like pie.
>   When the leaves turn red
>   I like to stay in bed."

"That was fine, Francine," Mrs. McGeltner said. Then she turned to Dixie. "Now, Dixie, let us hear your poem."

Dixie stood beside her desk and began to read.

> "When the tree outside my room
>   Scratches at my window,
>   It's saying, 'Come outside, come outside!'

The moon smiles through the glass,
Whispering, 'Come and go with me!'
And the wind whispers in a soft voice,
'Leave it all—go with me to the far West!'
But I lie in my bed and say,
'No, I will not let you in, Tree,
And I will not go with you, Moon,
And I will not go with you, Wind.'
But some night I will go.
I will go with the moon and the wind,
And then I will see what lies
So far beyond the tall mountains."

"Very nice, Dixie," Mrs. McGeltner said approvingly. "Class, let's talk for a while about Dixie's poem. It's a different kind of poem, isn't it? What do you think of it?"

"I think it doesn't make any sense," Francine said.

"Yeah, it didn't even rhyme!" Billy Joe added.

"It makes sense to anybody who's *got* sense, and a poem doesn't have to rhyme to be a poem!" Dixie said crossly.

Francine Mosely's face turned red. "Are you saying I don't have any sense?" she yelled.

"Girls! Girls!" Mrs. McGeltner exclaimed.

Dixie cried, "If you can understand what I just said, you ought to be able to understand the poem!"

"You're calling me stupid?" Francine leaned across the aisle and slapped Dixie's face.

Without thinking, Dixie grabbed Francine's hair.

"*Ow!*" Francine screeched.

"*Girls! Girls!*" Mrs. McGeltner cried louder.

Suddenly both girls were slapping and pulling hair.

"Girls! Stop that at once!" Mrs. McGeltner might as well have been talking to the April sun for all the good it did. She ran down the aisle. "Stop it! Both of you, stop it this minute!"

"She started it!" Dixie cried.

"Apologize to Francine, Dixie."

Dixie blinked. "She hit me first!"

"You provoked her, Dixie! You shouldn't suggest that anyone is stupid!"

"I didn't say she was. And she shouldn't have said my poem was dumb!"

"Very true . . ."

But Dixie soon found herself sitting on a chair outside the principal's office. She burned with indignation. She knew she deserved to be there, but it seemed Mrs. McGeltner had not been fair.

"Just because Francine's dad's got loads of money doesn't give her the right to get out of coming to the principal's office," she muttered.

The door opened, and Mr. Jones looked out. "Well, Dixie, what is it?"

Dixie slowly rose. "I had a fight, and Mrs. McGeltner sent me to see you."

Mr. Jones lifted one eyebrow. "Who did you fight with? I don't see anybody else here."

"Francine Mosely."

A frown creased the principal's brow. He glanced down the hall. "Well, come inside, and we'll talk it over."

With a sigh he shut the door behind them.

Leslie Stone caught up with Dixie after school. "What did he say?"

"I've got to write an essay on why I shouldn't pull anybody's hair."

"It's not fair!" Leslie said indignantly. "Francine ought to have to write an essay, too!"

"I could see Mr. Jones didn't like it. But you know how much influence the Moselys have around here. Don't worry about it, Leslie. I'll live."

Dixie got on the bus and took a seat in the back. As usual, most of the kids were screaming like banshees, but she paid no attention. Resentment boiled inside her as the yellow bus trundled along.

When she got off at her stop, the driver asked, "Somebody hurt your feelings, Dixie?"

She shook her head. "See you tomorrow, Mr. Melton," she muttered and went down the steps. Then she trudged along the stretch of road that led to the Snyder farm.

Dixie was helping take care of Aunt Edith, who'd been sick. And Uncle Roy and Aunt Edith were taking care of Dixie while her parents were in far-off Africa. For a moment she had trouble swallowing. But then she thought, *It won't be long now. As soon as they get a house built, they'll send for me. Then we'll all be together again, and won't I have fun in Africa!*

She found her aunt ironing. She looked pale.

"You shouldn't be doing that, Aunt

Edith! I'll do it. I'm not very good at iron-ing, but I'll be real careful."

"I get so tired of doing nothing," her aunt said.

"Why don't you just sit down? We'll both watch TV while I iron."

Aunt Edith protested, but in the end that's the way it was.

Then Dixie said, "Aunt Edith, maybe you should go and lie down while I fix sup-per."

"I think I will," her aunt agreed.

Dixie decided on noodles and pork chops and went to work.

"Supper's about ready, Uncle Roy," she said when her uncle came in from the fields.

When her aunt and uncle sat down, Dixie placed a bowl of noodles and a platter of pork chops on the table. She served creamed corn and a salad too.

"Well, this looks great!" Uncle Roy said after the blessing. He began to eat hungrily. "Anything happen at school today?"

For one moment Dixie had the notion of keeping the Francine incident secret. But it was impossible to keep anything a secret in Milo. Someone was sure to tell them. And anyway, she didn't want to deceive her aunt and uncle.

"I got sent to the principal's office."

A startled look appeared on both faces, and she quickly told the story.

"Well, I'm sorry to hear all that," Uncle Roy said. "Let me hear the poem."

"You want to hear the *poem?*"

"Sure, let's hear it!"

Dixie went to the living room and took a piece of paper from her notebook. She read the poem aloud and then looked over at them, waiting for their judgment.

"I think that's a great poem!" Uncle Roy said.

"I think so, too, Dixie."

"You mean you understand it?"

"Why, sure, we understand it!"

"But I wish you hadn't gotten into a fight with that girl," Aunt Edith said gently.

"Well, she hit me first!" Actually Dixie was ashamed of herself. Then she said, "It wasn't right of me to yank her hair like that, though. But she's so mean."

"I guess we all have our failings," Uncle Roy said. "What did the principal say?"

"He said I had to write an essay on why I shouldn't pull anybody's hair."

"That's not too bad," he said cheerfully. "I'll write it for you if you want me to."

Dixie giggled. "No, that's all right, Uncle Roy. I'll write it myself."

"Well, you run along. I'll do the dishes for Aunt Edith this time. Why don't you go see if you can catch us some perch out of the river?"

Dixie flashed him a smile. He always understood what she needed. "That's nice of you, Uncle Roy. I would like to go fishing."

"Go on and have a good time. Just be back before dark."

Dixie ran upstairs to change into a pair of cutoffs and an old T-shirt. Then she stuck her feet into some worn Nikes.

She always kept some worms for bait out in the barn. She threw a handful into a bucket, grabbed her pole and stringer, and made for the river, almost a mile away. It was always fun to go fishing. She not only liked to fish, but she liked the quietness too.

As soon as Dixie left her uncle's field, she was in deep woods. The afternoon shadows were starting to grow long. She wouldn't have much fishing time left by the time she got to the river.

Soon she passed an old deserted house. It sat in the middle of a field that had once been cultivated but now grew weeds.

I think I'll just stop at the pond here instead of going all the way to the river, she thought. She went around the house and over a crest and soon was seated under the hickory that shaded what had been an old stock pond.

She fished and let the silence sink into her, thinking mostly about Africa and her parents and how it would be when she got there. She thought of the circus too—of Aunt Sarah, the circus veterinarian, and of her friends there. She felt a little lonesome for them.

Finally, noting that it would start to get dark before long, she pulled up the stringer and counted the bream—eleven fish, all big and fat.

"That'll be plenty for supper tomorrow night," she murmured with satisfaction.

She hiked back over the ridge and was cutting through the trees that bordered the deserted house when a hand grabbed her arm and a voice shouted, *"What are you doing here?"*

Frightened out of her wits by the suddenness of it all, Dixie dropped both fish and pole and tried desperately to get away. "Let me go!"

The hand held her arm tightly, though. "I said, what are you doing here?"

Dixie lost some of her fear when she saw that it was just a boy about her own age. He was wearing a blue-checked shirt that was too big for him, a pair of frayed jeans, and a baseball cap on top of his curly black hair.

"Let me go!" She jerked away this time. "You're trespassing!"

"What are you talking about?" Dixie said. "Nobody lives here!"

"Yes, they do! Me and my family, we live here!"

Dixie gaped in disbelief. "I didn't hear about anybody buying this place!"

"Well, you're hearing about it now! What's your name?"

"Dixie Morris. What's yours?"

"My name's Manny Romanos." He jerked his head toward the house. "My mama and papa live there and also my two sisters and my brother and me. Now, if you got all the information you need, you can get off our place!"

"Why are you so mad?"

Manny Romanos scowled. "I'm just telling you what you'd tell me if you found me on *your* place!"

"That's not so!" Dixie said. "Why would I tell you to get off?"

"I been told to get off of enough places to know what it's like. Nobody likes gypsies."

"Are you a *gypsy?*" she asked. "I don't think I ever met a gypsy before."

"Well, you've met one now!"

"How old are you?"

"What do you care?"

"You're not much older than I am, and I'm eleven."

Manny Romanos shrugged. "I'm eleven, too. Now, you want to hear about my favorite foods and my favorite TV show?"

"How come I haven't met you in school?"

"Because I don't go to school."

"But you have to go to school. It's the law!"

The boy pulled his cap down firmly over his forehead. "I ain't got time to stand out here arguing with you!" He looked down at the fish. "You caught those fish out of our pond. They belong to me!"

Dixie wanted to grow angry, but she knew she had already lost her temper too many times that day. She handed the stringer to him. "Here," she said pleasantly. "You're welcome to them." She picked up the pole. "I'll see you later."

"Thanks for the warning!" Manny growled.

When Dixie got home, she put up her pole and bait can and went to where her uncle and aunt were sitting on the front porch.

"Guess what? I just met a gypsy!" she announced. She perched herself on the porch rail and told them about her encounter with Manny Romanos.

"Oh, dear!" Aunt Edith said anxiously. "I hate to hear that!"

"Hate to hear what?" Dixie asked.

"That *gypsies* have bought the old Benton place."

"What's wrong with gypsies?"

Uncle Roy shifted his weight on the porch swing. It creaked as he moved it back and forth. "Well, some people think gypsies are not very trustworthy. They're supposed to be people that steal quite a bit."

Dixie thought about that for a moment. "He *wasn't* very friendly," she admitted.

"I think it might be best," Aunt Edith said, "if you don't have anything to do with them. Perhaps they're just renting the place and won't stay there long."

"Might be best," Uncle Roy agreed.

Dixie said, "He'd have looked nice if he hadn't been so mad. He had pretty eyes for a boy."

Uncle Roy laughed. "So you're stuck on a pretty-eyed gypsy boy, are you?"

Dixie flushed. She knew her uncle liked to tease. She slid off the rail and walked away from the porch.

2
"NEVER TRUST A GYPSY!"

Dixie looked around the small room where her Sunday school class met each week. She thought, *I see the same people here as I see in English class.*

Her eyes went to Ollie and Patty Peck, whose father was the sheriff. She thought for a moment how much they looked like their dad, with their black hair and dark eyes.

Her gaze moved to Leslie and Kelly Stone, the pastor's daughter and son. Both had light hair and blue eyes. She liked them both.

But then Dixie's eyes reached the boy and girl who sat in a corner as far away from the teacher as they could. Billy Joe Satterfield was just as obnoxious in Sunday school as he was in English class.

Next to him was Francine Mosely, wearing an expensive dress, as usual. Dixie knew it was expensive. She had seen the price tag on it the last time she had visited the mall.

Mrs. Stone, the pastor's wife, was a good Sunday school teacher. Dixie listened as she began.

"A man once asked the Lord Jesus, 'Who is my neighbor?'"

"Why would he ask *that?*" Billy Joe interrupted. "I know all my neighbors. Why didn't he know his?"

"But being a neighbor doesn't always have to do with who lives in the house next door or on the farm next to ours," Mrs. Stone said patiently.

"Well, I know all *my* neighbors," Billy Joe repeated. "Don't care for some of them, either."

"And that's exactly what the story's about."

Mrs. Stone told the story. A traveler was beaten by robbers and left for dead. Another traveler came by, but he just went past on the other side of the road. Somebody else came along, and he also wouldn't help.

"But then," Mrs. Stone said, "some-body else saw him. He felt sorry for him. He bandaged his wounds. He took him to an inn and paid for all of his care. And when Jesus finished the story, He asked, 'Who was a neighbor to the man who fell into the robbers' hands?'"

"I know," Dixie said. "It was the Good Samaritan."

"And, Dixie, why was that?"

"Because he showed kindness to some-one when they needed it."

"So when *we* see someone in trouble— no matter who it is—we are to help."

Billy Joe said loudly, "You couldn't stop and help somebody today! You might get mugged!"

Francine put in her two cents' worth. "He's right. God gave us common sense, didn't He?"

"But Jesus isn't talking about common sense in this story. He's teaching us to be compassionate, even to people who are dif-ferent from us. You see, the Samaritans were hated in those days. Jewish people wouldn't have anything to do with them. The man who was robbed was Jewish—he was different from the Samaritan man. But the Samaritan helped him anyway."

Dixie remembered how many different kinds of people there had been when she was with the circus. She had learned to get along with all of them.

After Sunday school, the class walked to the auditorium for the sermon.

On the way, Ollie Peck got into an argument with Billy Joe Satterfield, which was not unusual. Ollie said, "That was a good Sunday school lesson! I don't care what you say, Billy Joe!"

"Well, I haven't noticed you being too kind to *me!* If I got beat up, you'd pass by on the other side of the road just like those guys in the story."

"I would not!"

"You two hush," Dixie said quickly. "You don't do anything but argue!"

"Well, who died and made you queen?" Billy Joe said. He whacked Dixie on the arm.

He probably intended it to be a playful gesture, but it really hurt. Dixie flared up before she thought. "If I found you all beat up, I probably *would* want to let you just lie there!"

"See, Sunday school doesn't do this one any good at all, even if she is a preacher's kid!"

And Dixie knew she had made a sad error.

After church, she passed Francine standing outside with her parents. Mr. Mosely was a big man. Francine's mother was little and pretty.

"Did you ask everyone to the swimming party, Francine?" she was saying.

Francine tightened her lips and looked straight at Dixie.

She had not asked Dixie, but now, Dixie thought, Francine knew she would have to.

"I forgot to tell you, Dixie," Francine said. "We're having a swimming party at my house this afternoon. I suppose it's too late to ask you . . ."

Earlier on, Dixie would have been hurt, but she had learned to put up with Francine. Knowing that Francine didn't want her to come, she smiled brilliantly. "Why, I'd love to come! Just let me go check with my aunt and uncle." She saw a frown cross Francine's face and almost laughed aloud. "I'll be right back," she said. "I'm sure they won't mind."

The swimming pool at the Mosely house was enormous. It was long enough to swim laps in, which Mr. Mosely was doing, thrashing the blue green water from one end to the other. The boys and girls gathered over on the other side to stay out of his path.

"Doesn't he ever get tired?" Kelly asked.

"Oh, he says it keeps him healthy," Francine said. She was wearing a silky new swimsuit.

Dixie was wearing last year's model. Now that she was here, she was sorry she had come.

Kids splashed and yelled. The boys shoved each other in. They threatened to shove the girls in. Dixie was practicing her dive.

"That's great!" Ollie said, after she made another clean dive. He was waiting when she swam to the side.

"You do OK yourself, Ollie. Let's take turns."

But at that moment Francine announced, "Everybody get dressed. We're going to listen to records. Hurry up! I'll see that the refreshments are ready by the time you get to the game room."

"She sure is bossy!" Ollie grumbled.

"Maybe it's worth being bossed around just to get to swim in a nice pool like this," Dixie said.

Soon everyone was dried off, dressed, and sitting in the Moselys' game room. It had a Ping-Pong table, and along the sides were all kinds of exercise machines. At the back was a real soda fountain.

Grinning, Billy Joe plopped himself down on one of the tall chairs. "I'll have a chocolate shake."

The Mosleys' maid gave him a disgusted look but said only, "All right. And what will the rest of you have?"

Dixie waited until the others had ordered. Then she said, "I'd like a chocolate sundae, if it wouldn't be too much trouble."

The maid smiled. She had been getting orders in less polite form. "No trouble at all. I'll fix you a real nice one."

"This is neat, Francine," Leslie said as they finished their shakes and sundaes. "Wish I had *my* own ice cream parlor!"

But Francine seemed to take it for granted that she should have an ice cream parlor in her house. And then Francine said, "All right, everybody hurry up! I want to take you down and give you a demonstration of riding!"

"Oh, no!" Ollie moaned. "Now we've got to watch her ride that horse of hers."

"Well, it *is* a pretty horse," Dixie said.

Francine marched everybody toward the pasture. By the time they got there, she had informed them how much the horse had cost and how much better he was than any other horse. However, when she got to the edge of the field, she looked around, puzzled. "He's not here!"

"Maybe he's in the barn," Patty Peck said.

"Not usually. He likes to be outside."

However, Francine ran to the barn and looked inside. She was back in a moment, alarm in her eyes. "He's not there, either! He must have gotten out!"

A quick search was made. No horse was found.

Everybody ran back to the house, where they found Mr. Mosely on the patio talking to his brother.

Lester Mosely was a gangly man with a brown ponytail. He lived by himself on a run-down farm a few miles away.

"Thunder's gone, Daddy!" Francine cried.

"He was there this morning."

"I don't care! He's not there now!"

"Well, let's go have a look." Mr. Mosely and his brother led the way, first to the pasture and then to the barn.

Lester said, "Somebody's stolen that horse."

"Nonsense!" Mr. Mosely said. "Who'd steal a horse these days? There haven't been any horse thieves since the days of the Old West!"

"Well, let's see if we can find some tracks. The ground's damp."

Quickly they spread out, looking, and soon Lester yelled, "Here! Here's some tracks! They're not hard to follow."

"The horse probably just wandered off," Mr. Mosely said.

The group started through the woods. Francine kept calling, "Thunder! Come here, Thunder!"

They had walked almost a half mile when suddenly Francine said, "There he is!"

Dixie saw a boy coming, leading a horse. And she realized with a shock that it was Manny Romanos, the gypsy boy.

As soon as they were close enough, Francine demanded, "What are you doing with my horse?"

Lester Mosely looked angry, too. He grabbed the rope about the horse's neck. "Who are you, kid?"

Manny was wearing the same clothes that he had worn when Dixie first saw him. He had a hat pulled down over resentful eyes. "I found him. I was bringing him home."

"I ain't seen you around here," Lester said. "What's your name?"

"Manny Romanos."

"Where do you live?"

Dixie said, "His family bought the old Benton place over close to us."

Then Francine said, "What are you?"

"What do you mean, what am I?" Manny said, lifting his head. "I'm a boy. What are *you*?"

Francine's face grew red. "He was stealing Thunder, Daddy! Let's take him to Sheriff Peck and have him arrested."

"Hold on, now!" Mr. Mosely said. "We

don't know that." He looked down at Manny. "You say you found this horse?"

"He was loose out in the woods, and I put a rope around his neck, and I followed his tracks back this way."

"You're some kind of a gypsy, ain't you?" Lester said.

"We're Romanies," Manny answered.

Lester sneered. "You can call yourself anything you want, but you ain't nothin' but a gypsy!"

Dixie said, "It was nice of you to bring the horse back, Manny."

"Bring him back? He was stealing him!" Francine said. "Daddy, aren't you going to have him arrested?"

"Why should we? You've got your horse back, and that's the important thing."

"If it was *my* horse, *I'd* have him arrested," Lester said. "You can never trust a gypsy!"

For some reason, Dixie felt defensive. "Why are you picking on him?"

"These people ain't like us," Lester said. He was beginning to sound like Francine. "Everybody knows gypsies steal—especially horses—whenever they can!"

"I never stole this horse!" Manny turned and walked off.

Francine called after him, "You'd better stay away from this place! You ever come around here again, you'll be sorry!"

"That's enough, Francine," her father said. "We don't know he stole the horse!"

Lester did most of the talking on the way back. He claimed to have had a great deal of experience with gypsies, all bad. Francine agreed with everything he said.

Suddenly Ollie said, "You didn't pay much attention to the Sunday school lesson, did you, Francine?"

"Now what are you talking about?"

"It was about being nice to people who are different from us. That gypsy boy sure is different. You weren't very nice to him."

Francine snapped, "If it had been your horse he'd stolen, you wouldn't be so easy on him."

Dixie said nothing. She kept remembering the hurt in the boy's eyes.

That night she told her uncle and aunt what happened. "Think how he must have felt. He was doing a good deed by bringing the horse back. Instead of being thanked, he got accused of stealing it. It's not fair."

Aunt Edith said nervously, "Well, gypsies do have a bad reputation, Dixie."

While Dixie washed the dishes, she was still thinking about Manny Romanos. She thought about him until she went to bed.

As she lay there, she began to pray, "Lord, I don't know whether Manny stole the horse, but I know he wasn't treated fairly. So I ask that You bless Manny and his family. In Jesus' name, Amen."

3
A CHANGE OF MIND

Rumors about horse stealing spread around the small village of Milo as quickly as a radio dispatch.

One of the chief dispatchers was Minnie Stokes. A bony woman with gray hair and alert brown eyes, she served as a walking, talking, living, breathing gossip column for the whole town.

Mrs. Stokes arrived at the Snyder home early the next morning.

Dixie had just cut her pancakes into bite-sized morsels when the doorbell rang. She went to the front door. "Oh, hello, Mrs. Stokes."

"Dixie, are your uncle and aunt free?"

"Well, we're eating breakfast. Come on in."

Dixie led the woman into the dining room. "Mrs. Stokes has come for a visit."

A quick look of displeasure swept across Uncle Roy's face. But getting up, he said, "Sit down, Minnie. Have some breakfast."

"Oh, no, I couldn't do that!" Mrs. Stokes protested.

Aunt Edith said, "You can at least have a cup of coffee."

Dixie took a mug from the cupboard. She filled it with coffee, set it before Mrs. Stokes, and returned to her pancakes.

"It's just the *awfulest* thing, isn't it?"

"What's awful, Minnie?" Aunt Edith said tiredly. Dixie knew that, like Uncle Roy, she had little sympathy for Minnie Stokes.

"Why, the gypsy that stole Mr. Mosely's horse!"

Dixie swallowed her bite of pancake. "That's not what happened, though, Mrs. Stokes," she said. "Manny found the horse in the woods. He was bringing it back."

"That's not the way I heard it!" Mrs. Stokes gave her a severe look. "And who is this *Manny?*"

"His family bought the Benton place."

After that, Minnie Stokes paid no attention at all to Dixie. She turned to the adults and told how, when she was a girl, some gypsies had come by and afterwards the family had missed some clothes that had been hanging on the line.

Finally, Mrs. Stokes got up to go. She said, "Be sure you keep your doors locked at night."

Dixie led her to the front door. "Good-bye, Mrs. Stokes."

When she got back to the dining room, her uncle and aunt were talking about the gypsies. Dixie plopped down into her chair. "It's not true what she's saying. Manny wouldn't steal anything!"

"Well, you really don't know him, dear," Aunt Edith said.

"I do know him! I met him!" Dixie did not mention Manny's being unfriendly with her. Instead, she said, "I'm going to take them some brownies and welcome them to the neighborhood."

"Would that be wise?" Aunt Edith asked.

"Oh, let her go, Edith!" Uncle Roy said. "If they're going to be our neighbors, that would be a nice gesture."

As soon as Dixie had washed the dishes, she began to make brownies. Since she was in a hurry, she just used a mix this time. Soon the kitchen was filled with the delicious aroma of brownies baking.

Soon Dixie was on her bicycle, pedaling down the road. The brownies were in a grocery sack in her bike basket. It was a fine day.

At the Romanos house, she got off and began pushing the bicycle. Now that she was here, she wasn't sure that she was doing the right thing.

"Maybe they won't like me," she murmured. But she had come this far, and she would go through with it.

Dixie was relieved when Manny himself appeared at the door. But he had a strange expression in his eyes, and he scowled. "Come to arrest me?"

Dixie put down the bike's kickstand. Then she took the paper sack from the basket. "No, I didn't come for that," she said. "I've come to welcome you into the neighborhood and to meet your family."

Just as she said this, the house seemed to erupt.

A man and a woman came out the door first.

The man—Manny's father?—was wearing a soft hat with a wide brim, a crimson shirt, and a pair of checkered trousers. He wore half-boots too, and around his neck was a brilliant emerald green scarf. He had a long, sweeping black mustache. But what caught Dixie's attention the most was the enormous gold earring hanging from his left ear.

"Well, and who is this come to visit?"

"My name is Dixie Morris. I met Manny and came to welcome you into the neighborhood. We live down this road about three miles."

"Ah, it is nice you come for visit!" Mr. Romanos's teeth were white against his dark complexion. He had a very nice smile. "I am Victor Romanos, and this is my wife, Maria."

Mrs. Romanos had black hair and dark eyes. She was wearing gold earrings and a rose-colored dress that came down to her ankles. Her smile was as nice as her husband's.

She said, "These are our other children. This is Rolf, and this is Sonia."

Rolf looked to be about five and Sonia eight. Both were dressed much like their parents.

"And this is Emily." Mrs. Romanos turned to a toddler who had just emerged. She was small and chubby and had the black hair of the rest of the family.

"Oh, she's darling!" Dixie cried. "Emily, do you like brownies?"

Emily did not seem to be bashful. She said, "Yes."

Dixie took out the sack of brownies and opened it. Emily promptly took one and began cramming it into her mouth.

Then Dixie took the sack to her mother.

Mrs. Romanos accepted the brownies and began passing them around. When she came to Manny, he took one bite, then nodded. "Real good."

"'Real good'! That's the best you can say?" Mr. Romanos kissed his fingertips. He made a graceful bow. "I have *never* tasted better brownies!"

Rolf reached for another one, but his mother slapped his hand. "Enough! We will take our guest inside and offer her some refreshments. Do you like tea or coffee, Dixie?"

"Well, I like coffee, but you don't have to make it just for me."

"You are our guest," Mr. Romanos said. "Come inside. We welcome you into our home."

Dixie had been in the small house before—she and Ollie Peck had once gone in through a window and had played games inside. The place had been rundown then, so now she gasped with surprise.

"You've done such a good job of fixing up the place, Mrs. Romanos!"

A couch was covered with a blue blanket. There were three straight-backed wooden chairs, a small table, and a lamp. The walls were decorated with bright-colored pictures. Handmade rag rugs lay on the worn wooden floors.

"We have waited a long time for a home," Mrs. Romanos said. "We've traveled all over the country in our *vardot*."

"What's a *vardot*?"

"You don't know what a *vardot* is?" Manny said. He went to the window and gestured.

Looking out, Dixie saw what looked like a red, green, and yellow circus wagon. There were no horses attached to it, but it was obviously meant to be horse-drawn. It had a small window on each side and doors in the front and back.

Dixie exclaimed, "Why, that's the prettiest wagon I've ever seen!"

"Not wagon. *Vardot!*" Manny insisted.

"Let her call it a wagon if she wants to, Manny!" Mrs. Romanos admonished him. "Here, you sit down, Dixie, and I will make the coffee."

Dixie kept looking around the room as Mr. Romanos talked about their travels. It seemed they had been back and forth across the United States many times.

"It is good to travel," he said. "All Romanies like to travel."

"What are Romanies?" Dixie asked.

"What you call gypsies. We call ourselves Romanies, though."

"I'll remember that," Dixie said. "Won't you be traveling anymore?"

"Oh, yes. We like to travel, but we need a permanent place too. We saved money for a long time to buy this house. Now we will travel in the summer, and this will be our winter home."

"Well, welcome. I'm anxious for you to meet my uncle and aunt. You'll like them."

Manny said, "I didn't like the *Moselys!*"

Silence fell over the room.

Then Dixie said, "I'm sure there's some mistake there. Actually, Mr. Mosely's a nice man."

"Who is this *Lester* Mosely?" Manny demanded.

"He's Mr. Mosely's younger brother. He's not quite as nice as Mr. George Mosely."

When the coffee was poured, everybody ate brownies again. Then Mr. Romanos took down a violin from a peg on the wall. "You like music?"

"I love music."

"Good. I'll play a song just for you, our first guest in our new home."

He tucked the violin under his chin, his fingers began to fly, and the bow flew across the strings. It was a nice tune, and she applauded when he was through. "What's the name of that?"

"It's called 'Song for Dixie.'"

Dixie stared. "You mean you just made it up?"

"Oh, he makes up songs for everything that happens," Mrs. Romanos said.

"I think that's wonderful!"

Dixie listened to Mr. Romanos play two

more songs. Then she said, "I'd better go now. My aunt's not well, and I don't like to leave her alone for too long."

"We are honored that you should come to our house." Mr. Romanos bowed again.

"I'll walk a ways with you," Manny said.

She said as she left, "Thank you for the coffee. It was very good. My uncle will come by to visit soon, and I hope you can come to see us."

Instead of riding her bike, Dixie pushed it, and Manny walked along beside her.

Suddenly he said, "I thought I was going to hate it here."

"But why?"

"Because most people don't like Romanies."

Dixie could not think of anything to say. "I've never known any Romanies before," she said at last, "but your family is very nice!"

"Well, it was good of you to come over. Not many people would do that."

"Some nice people live around here, Manny, and when you start in school you'll meet some more kids."

All of a sudden, the sound of a horse neighing caught Dixie's attention. She turned and saw a beautiful chestnut. He was stretching his neck over a fence, obviously trying to catch their attention.

"All right, Champ, I see you," Manny called.

"Is that *your* horse?"

"Sure. His name's Champion. I just call him Champ."

"Could I pet him?"

"Why, yeah. Yeah, you can pet him."

Dixie laid down her bicycle, and they walked to the fence. The horse arched his head over the wire, and Manny rubbed his nose. "Now he won't bite you," he said.

"I spent a lot of time with a circus. I'm not afraid of animals. Oh, he's so beautiful!" She rubbed the silken nose, and Champ nibbled at her fingers. "I wish I'd brought an apple for him. I'll do that next time."

Manny stroked Champ's neck. Then he said abruptly, "I'm going to train him and sell him to make some money to help my family."

"What are you going to train him to do?"

"I don't know yet. He's a quarter horse. They can be trained to do almost anything."

Dixie said, "He sure is beautiful! Do you suppose I could ride him?"

"What if you fall off? Your relatives would blame me."

"I won't fall off!" Dixie said indignantly. "I rode in the circus parade three times a day sometimes! I never fell off once! Sometimes I even rode an elephant, and I never fell off her, either!"

"You rode an elephant in a circus parade? Wow. Wish I could do that!"

"Let me ride him!"

"Well . . . we could ride together, I guess . . ."

Soon they were astride the chestnut. Dixie sat behind, holding onto Manny.

"Can you make him gallop?"

"Without a saddle?"

"Sure! In the circus they ride bareback all the time. I didn't do much of that, but I had a friend who did."

"Well, come on, Champ, let's show this *Gorgio* what a real horse is like."

"*Gorgio?* That's a kind of perfume!"

"That's what we call people who aren't Romanies."

"Oh, I didn't know that!"

The ride was a lot of fun for Dixie. She missed riding the circus horses and the elephant Ruth. When they trotted back, she slid to the ground, saying again, "He's a beautiful horse, Manny. You must be very proud of him."

"You ride good," he answered. "Not many girls could get on a horse without a saddle and stay on!"

Dixie was pleased. She said, "Maybe the next time I come you'll let me ride him again."

"Maybe."

Dixie got on her bicycle. "See you later, Manny. I enjoyed the visit."

"Yeah, me too."

When Dixie got home, she found Uncle Roy working in the garden. She excitedly related what had happened.

"They sound like nice people," he said.

"They are. Do you think we can have them over to supper sometime?"

"If you do the cooking, I don't see why not. They wouldn't want to eat mine."

"Oh, I'd do that." Dixie nodded eagerly. "Now I'm going in and write Mom and Dad and tell them all about my new friends."

Dixie soon was sitting at her desk in her room, writing busily. Her letter was full of her encounter with the Romanies. She finished by saying, "They are such nice-looking people. And nice-acting." Then she added a PS: "I think I'm going to be very fond of the Romanos family. I hope people are nice to them."

4

NEW STUDENTS

Who's that getting off the bus with Dixie?"

Francine Mosely looked up and narrowed her eyes. "It's that gypsy boy—the one that stole my horse! He ought to be in jail!"

Billy Joe Satterfield laughed. "We got a rustler right here in Milo. Just like the Old West!"

They watched Dixie cross the schoolyard accompanied by Manny Romanos and somebody who was probably his sister.

Dixie saw Manny and Sonia when she got on the school bus. Smiling, she went to sit behind them, saying, "I'm glad we can ride the same bus on your first day at school."

Manny said only, "Yeah, I guess so." Sonia seemed too frightened to say anything.

Dixie chattered all the way about what a good school it was and how much fun they would have.

Sonia was not wearing her Romany outfit but a nice dress that looked brand-new. When Dixie commented on it, she nodded. "Mama bought it for me to wear to school."

As they approached the schoolhouse entrance, Dixie said, "First, we'll find Sonia's teacher."

"Papa came with us yesterday," Sonia said. She still looked frightened. "But all these kids weren't here then."

"In a week you'll know most of them," Dixie said cheerfully.

"Hey, gypsy, I need my fortune told!"

Billy Joe Satterfield and Francine Mosely were standing at the door. He held out his big hand toward Sonia and grinned. "Come on, give me a good one, now! Am I going to take a long journey and meet a beautiful woman?"

Sonia looked even more frightened. She drew closer to Manny.

Manny said gruffly, "Put your hand down, or I'll cut it off for you!"

"Oh, that's right! Gypsies carry knives, don't they?"

"Billy Joe Satterfield, you be quiet!" Dixie put her hand on Billy Joe's chest and pushed him backward.

"Hey, don't get sore, Dixie. I was just kidding!" Billy Joe winked at Francine.

Now other kids gathered around. Dixie saw Ollie Peck and his sister coming. She always felt better when Ollie and Patty were there.

And then she saw Leslie and Kelly Stone crossing the schoolyard. They were good friends, too, so she called out, "Leslie, I want you to meet somebody."

Dixie waited until Leslie and Kelly were close. Then she said, loudly enough for everybody within twenty yards to hear, "We've got some new kids coming to school. This is Manny Romanos and his sister, Sonia. They're special friends of mine, and I want you all to give them a good welcome."

Both Leslie and Kelly smiled and said it was good to have new students. Ollie said, "Hey, Manny, can you play basketball? We need another guy on our team."

"I'm not much good," Manny said.

"Oh, that's all right," Ollie said cheerfully. "I'm not much good either, but it's fun!"

"There's the first bell," Patty said.

"Have you got your schedule, Manny? What's your first class?" Dixie asked as they headed for the door.

"It's English."

"Oh, that's good," Dixie said. "We'll be in class together! Let's take Sonia down to her room first."

In the third-grade room, Mrs. Williams greeted Sonia with a smile, and Dixie saw, with relief, that although the children stared curiously at the newcomer, they weren't unfriendly. She whispered to Sonia, "I'll see you at lunch. You and Manny and I can eat together in the cafeteria." She gave the girl a hug. "You're going to make lots of friends here."

"All right, if you say so."

Dixie joined Manny in the hall. "The English room is one-oh-six. It's right down here. Now, you mustn't mind Mrs. McGeltner. She's crabby sometimes!"

"Don't you like her?"

"Well, she doesn't really try to get people to like her," Dixie said. "Not like a lot of the teachers around here. Now, you take Miss Johnson, the science teacher . . ."

She continued her rundown of the teachers until they went into the classroom. "Mrs. McGeltner, this is Manny Romanos. His family's moved in down the road from us."

Mrs. McGeltner peered at Manny over her glasses and nodded briefly. But she was not unkind as she said, "I hope you do well in English class, Manny. Do you like English?"

Manny shifted uncertainly. He looked at the floor, then he looked up, shrugging. "I don't do too well," he admitted.

Mrs. McGeltner frowned a little. "Well, we'll have to help you do better. You may take that desk over there by the wall."

Manny obeyed. Then he sat stiffly and watched as the other students filed in.

Dixie saw him especially watching Billy Joe Satterfield and Francine Mosely. Billy Joe whispered something into Francine's ear. She giggled and nodded, and both of them stared at Manny.

"All right, class, come to order! I'm going to call the roll," Mrs. McGeltner said. "We have a new student today." She looked down at the name. "Manny Romanos. Say hello to Manny, class."

The class all said, "Hello, Manny."

He flushed slightly and lowered his head, looking at the desk in front of him.

Dixie hoped desperately that no one would make fun of him or mention the affair about the horse. But that was too good a chance for Billy Joe to pass up. She saw him whispering to his neighbors and then nodding toward Manny.

Mrs. McGeltner had enough of it. "Billy Joe, if you don't be quiet, I'll have you go down and see the principal."

Billy Joe merely grinned at her. "I was just talking about how we could welcome our new student. Maybe we could all put gold rings in our ears. Ain't that what gypsies do?"

"Some Romanies wear gold earrings," Manny piped up, but so do some *Gorgios.*"

"Hey, he's talking a foreign language! Romanies? *Gorgios?* What's that?"

"I am Romany! You are *Gorgio!* Anybody who is not a Romany is a *Gorgio!*"

Billy Joe cackled loudly. "Look at me, everybody. I'm a *Gorgio!* Francine, you're a *Gorgio!*"

"That will be enough, Billy Joe!" Mrs. McGeltner said. "Now, open your books to page eighty-nine. We're going to continue with our study of what poetry means, and I trust that we won't have another barbaric fight over the nature of poetry!"

Dixie thought Mrs. McGeltner looked directly at her as she said that.

"Today we'll study poetry by Robert Frost. The first poem is one called 'Mending Wall.' First, I will read it to you."

Mrs. McGeltner read the poem, which was one of the things she did very well. She had a clear voice and read with great feeling.

Dixie had read the poem before and liked it. It was about a man who set out to repair the stone wall on his farm. He did this simply by picking up stones that had fallen off the wall and replacing them.

Then Mrs. McGeltner asked, "Does anyone think you know what this poem means?"

"It's about a guy repairing a fence," Billy Joe said loudly.

"No, it's not about that!" Dixie spoke up at once. "I remember what you told us, Mrs. McGeltner—Robert Frost said a poem says one thing and means another."

Mrs. McGeltner was pleased at having herself quoted. "That's right. So there is a wall here, and a man is mending it, but what's it all about? What do you think, Dixie?"

"Well, at the last of the poem, the man that's helping the farmer build his wall back asks him why he wants a wall. There aren't any cows to keep in or anything, and the man just says good fences make good neighbors." Dixie thought hard. "I think the poem means that we don't need to build walls around ourselves to keep people out."

Again Mrs. McGeltner was pleased. "That's exactly what the poem means! The rock wall is just a symbol of other walls. Can you tell me what kind of walls we build? Anyone?"

Francine Mosely said, "I think you have to have walls, or people would come tramping into your life when you didn't want them."

"Right." Billy Joe grinned. "Can't just have anybody coming into your house, and a house is just a kind of wall."

Dixie argued that you didn't need to keep people out, and Francine and Billy Joe just as loudly argued that you did need to keep *some* people out.

Mrs. McGeltner seemed both pleased and surprised. It was usually very difficult to get *any* discussion about poetry. Finally the argument got so noisy that she held up her hand. "Please, students, I'm glad to see you interested in our subject . . ."

But Billy Joe was not to be put down. Dixie saw him wink at Francine, then look at Manny. "Hey, gypsy, what do you think about that? Don't you think we need to build some kind of walls to keep people out of our lives?"

"Billy Joe," Mrs. McGeltner said icily. "That's *enough.*"

Manny had been staring at his desk. He lifted his head slowly and said, "I don't know about poetry, but I know about being kept out. Everywhere me and my family go, it's like people build walls. Except for some."

Dixie flushed. She knew this was Manny's way of thanking her for being his friend.

Mrs. McGeltner said, "Well, that's all the time we have for this poem, class. Let me make an assignment for tomorrow . . ."

Lunch time seemed to be a welcome relief to Manny. When they met Sonia at the cafeteria, right away he asked, "How did it go, sister?"

"It was all right, Manny," Sonia said. "A girl in there likes me. Her name is Ruthie."

Dixie hugged Sonia. "See, I told you you'd find a friend! Now let's go chow down."

When they joined the line that led to the hot-food table, Manny said nervously, "I don't know how to do this."

"It's easy. You just tell them what you want for the main dish. Today you can have either a hamburger or stew."

"We eat stew all the time," Sonia said. "I'm going to have a hamburger."

"You just tell the lady, then."

Dixie guided them through the line—Manny also took a hamburger—and they walked to the table where Ollie and Patty were sitting.

"Sit down," Ollie said. "How'd it go, Manny?"

"All right, I guess."

"And did you do all right, too, Sonia?" Patty asked.

"Yes! I liked it better than any school I ever went to."

"Well, let's pray," Dixie said and saw confusion in the faces of the newcomers. "I'll say it this time." She bowed her head and said a short prayer. Then she said, "You can go back for seconds if you want more."

Sonia said, "I like hamburgers. I wish I could have them every day."

"You'd get tired of them." Patty smiled. "Anything we have every day gets old."

"Not for me," Ollie said. "I could eat strawberry shortcake every day and not get tired of it."

"Yes, you would!" Patty argued. "You got on an apple pie kick once. Mom baked apple pie three times in a row, and then you started griping because it wasn't chocolate!"

Their argument was friendly, and Manny and Sonia seemed to be relaxing.

But all was spoiled when Billy Joe came by, accompanied by two friends. He said loudly, "Here they are! These are the gypsies! They steal horses and tell fortunes!"

"That's a lie!" Manny said. He got to his feet, his face tense.

Dixie leaped up. "You get out of here,

Billy Joe! Don't you ever get tired of listening to yourself?"

Manny stood while Dixie shooed off Billy Joe and his friends. At last he sat back down.

"Never mind him!" Dixie said. "Tell us more about Champ."

Manny was clearly upset, but as he began to talk about his horse, he relaxed again.

Then the bell rang, and Dixie said, "Time for social science."

Unfortunately, social science class was spoiled by the fact that Francine and her little group of admirers were there. Fortunately, Billy Joe was not.

The teacher, Mrs. Simmons, was a pleasant lady. She seemed to know a great deal about many things. Almost at once, she introduced Manny.

"We like to find out a little bit about newcomers. It's a way to get acquainted quickly. That's what social science is about —people getting along." She smiled brightly. "Tell us about yourself, Manny. Let's start with hobbies. Do you have a hobby?"

Manny shifted uncomfortably and looked toward Dixie. "Yes. I'm training a quarter horse."

"Training him to do what?"

"I'm not sure," Manny said. "Maybe for calf roping or bulldogging. He'd make a good barrel racer too."

Francine said, "What do *you* know about barrel racing?"

Manny pressed his lips together.

Dixie raised her hand. "I know about barrel races. I went to a rodeo once and saw them. Girls get to do barrel racing." She hesitated, then said, "I think I'd like to try that—riding a horse around the barrels."

Francine laughed. "You'd fall off before you hit the first barrel! It's very difficult and takes great ability on the part of the rider!"

"Well, I think I could do it!"

"I'd like to see you try it."

"Maybe I will!"

"All right, girls . . ." Mrs. Simmons began.

Dixie knew she was talking out of turn, but she heard herself saying, "I bet I could learn to ride well enough to compete in a rodeo. Especially with a horse like Champ. Manny, would you let me practice on your horse?"

"Sure," he said.

"A gypsy's horse oughtn't be mentioned in the same breath as my horse," Francine said. "He's a thoroughbred!"

Mrs. Simmons stopped the discussion of hobbies at that point. "Well, I didn't intend for us to get into a disagreement about this . . ."

After class, Francine picked up her books. "Don't bother trying to learn to ride, Dixie," she said grandly. "You can't do it."

Dixie watched her leave and then turned to Manny. "You know what? When someone tells me I can't do something, it makes me want to."

Manny Romanos suddenly grinned. It was the biggest smile she had seen on his face since she'd met him.

"Though on second thought, it does sound pretty silly—me trying to learn to ride good enough for a rodeo."

"Why would you say that?"

"Well, it looks hard to do, and has Champ ever run the barrels?"

"No, but he's a smart horse. You and I could train him together. That'd make him more valuable when I get ready to sell him."

Dixie suddenly laughed. "All right, then. We'll do it! Here we come, rodeo! Dixie Morris riding Manny Romanos's horse, Champ. Look out, everybody!"

5

CHAMP DOES HIS STUFF

By the end of the week, Dixie had for certain made up her mind about learning to ride Champ. She'd said nothing yet to her uncle and aunt, but every day, on the bus and during lunch, she and Manny would talk about competing in a rodeo.

Dixie made waffles for breakfast on Saturday morning.

Uncle Roy speared a crispy morsel, put it into his mouth, then rolled his eyes. "Best waffle made on the face of the earth —or anywhere else, for that matter!"

Candy Sweet cut his waffle into four sections instead of small bites. "Best waffles I ever had, and I've been all the way to St. Louis."

Even Aunt Edith ate more than usual. She said, "Maybe I can start taking over some of the work now, Dixie."

"Don't rush yourself, Aunt Edith. You just take it easy."

"I don't know what we would have done without you, Dixie," Uncle Roy said. "We're mighty grateful we have a niece willing to pitch in and help like you have."

"Well, I was glad to do it."

Her uncle leaned back in his chair. "I know it must be a little boring around here for you—after all the exciting times you had with your Aunt Sarah at the circus."

Dixie got up, smiling. "Don't you worry. I'm having a good time here, and I'm going to have an even better time now."

"What do you mean?" Aunt Edith asked.

"I'm going to learn to ride Manny's horse. We're going to enter the rodeo and win some prizes."

"Isn't that dangerous?" Aunt Edith asked nervously.

"Not really. It'll be exciting. I'm going over this morning and get my first lesson."

"You go ahead, then, Dixie. I'll wash the dishes."

"Thanks, Uncle Roy." Dixie beamed.

She changed into jeans and a white T-shirt and a pair of old shoes and was soon bicycling toward the Romanos house.

When she pedaled into their yard, Sonia and Rolf greeted her, and Emily came toddling behind them.

"Hello," Dixie said. "Is Manny home?"

"Right here!" He came out of the house, followed by his mother. "Ready for your first lesson?" He wore a bright handkerchief around his neck, much like his father.

Mrs. Romanos smiled warmly. "I'm a little worried about you riding that horse, Dixie. Victor says he's a real handful."

Dixie grinned. "Well, after riding camels and an elephant and a tiger, I don't think I'll have any trouble with a horse."

"A tiger! Did you really ride a *tiger*, Dixie?" Sonia's mouth hung open.

"Sure did. His name was Stripes."

"Weren't you afraid?" Rolf asked, his eyes big.

"No, he was just like a big kitty cat."

"Well, he probably didn't travel as fast as Champ," Manny said. "A quarter horse can go pretty fast, and if you fall off, it's not much fun. I know. I've got the bruises to prove it."

"I'm not afraid," Dixie insisted.

"Have lunch with us today, Dixie,"

Manny's mother said. "See how Romanies eat."

"That sounds good to me. I'll let Aunt Edith know."

As Dixie and Manny walked down the path to the pasture, she suddenly asked, "Do you really think we can do this, Manny?"

"Sure, why not?"

"Oh, I'm always talking more than I should." She gave a half laugh. "Sometimes I talk when I should be listening."

Manny grinned. "Papa says I need to talk less and listen more."

"That's what my dad always said to me. I guess we're a whole lot alike."

"No, you're *Gorgio,* and I'm Romany."

Dixie didn't answer for a moment. Then she said, "I don't think you ought to talk like that. I mean—we're friends."

"Well, I've had some bad experiences." His face grew sober as they approached the small barn. "It *hurts* when people won't be friendly. That's why that poem kind of got to me—the poem where that guy said good fences make good neighbors. I don't think they do. I think they make bad neighbors."

"And I think you're right." Dixie would

have said more, but Manny apparently wanted to change the subject.

"Can you saddle a horse?" he asked.

"I've never tried."

"Well, you're about to get your first lesson."

Champ pitched a little, but Manny spoke to him in an authoritative tone. "You've got to show them who's boss," he said. "Now you be still, Champ!"

Champ turned, plucked Manny's hat off his head, and held it high.

"Give me that, you ornery horse!" But he laughed. And when the horse refused to give it back, he still just laughed. "All right, keep it then! Here, Dixie. First, you put the blanket on. Like this." He showed her how. "Then you throw the saddle over."

Dixie swung the heavy saddle but only managed to hit Champ in the side. He startled sideways, dropped the hat, gave her a wild-eyed look.

"Oh, I didn't mean to hurt him!" Dixie cried.

"You didn't hurt him. You just have to lift it higher. Let me saddle him this time. You can practice by putting the saddle on the fence rail."

That worked much better, and soon Champ was saddled and bridled.

"I found some old barrels at the dump, and Papa hauled them home," Manny said.

Dixie got on Champ, and soon they were approaching three barrels standing in the open field.

Manny explained how barrel racing worked. "You just ride the horse around the barrels. Rodeo arenas aren't always shaped alike, but there are always three barrels set in a triangle like they are here. This one here is at the start."

"So how do you win?"

"Well, it's a timed event," Manny said. "Only one rider competes at a time."

Dixie looked at the barrels, thinking, *I don't know if I can learn to do this!* But aloud she said, "Does it matter which way I go around them?"

"Most riders take the first barrel to the right, and they circle it clockwise. The next two they'll probably circle counterclockwise. The rules say that you've got to turn both ways during the run. And that's all there is to it."

"Doesn't *sound* too hard," Dixie said thoughtfully.

Manny peered up at her. "Nothing's hard if you know how to do it and have lots of practice. But it's awful easy to knock a barrel down. If you could just *walk* the horse around, there'd be nothing to it, and that's what we'll do right now. Go out and circle that first barrel clockwise. Then do the other two counterclockwise. Don't try to hurry."

Dixie looked at the barrels. "All right, I'll try. Get up, Champ!" She kicked the horse with her heels and released the reins.

Champ moved obediently along, swinging his head from side to side.

"Keep the reins tighter, so you can control him."

Dixie approached the first barrel. She sawed the horse's head around by pulling too hard, and he snorted and began to pitch. She grabbed for the saddle horn, and he calmed down, but when she looked back at Manny, he was laughing.

"You're not going to win any contests like that!"

"You just wait, Manny Romanos. I'll show you!"

All morning Manny worked with Dixie. Toward noon, he said, "That's enough now.

You don't want to tire the horse out." At the barn, he let her pull off the bridle, and then he did the unsaddling. "Let's go get something to eat. I'm starved."

"How do you think I did?"

"OK for a beginner. You're not afraid of horses. It's just going to take a lot of practice."

"I think it's fun." She looked over shyly and said, "It's good to have a partner."

Manny finally nodded. "Yeah, I guess so."

Back at the house, Dixie phoned Aunt Edith. Then she learned what a real gypsy meal was like. Mrs. Romanos had cooked stew in an iron pot over an outside fire.

She told Dixie, "This is the way we cook when we're on the road. Actually, I like it better inside. But somehow stew comes out better when I cook it in this big old black pot."

Mr. Romanos asked, "How did the horse-riding lesson go?"

"Well, I didn't fall off."

"That's good. You can't win unless you stay on."

Soon Dixie was sitting on a box in the yard, eating rich, juicy stew.

"What's in this?" she asked.

"This is Mama's special," Mr. Romanos said. "She puts everything she can find in it, so it's 'a little bit of everything stew.'"

"It's rabbit," Sonia said. "We trapped them. Did you ever snare a rabbit?"

"I never did. How do you do it?"

Dixie listened with interest as Sonia explained. Then she said, "I don't think I could kill a rabbit. I didn't think I could *eat* it, either, but I am!"

After the meal, Mr. Romanos brought out his fiddle and played song after song. Some of them she knew. Some she suspected he had made up.

"I've got to go home," she said at last. "I have to do the washing."

As she left, Manny asked, "Will you come back tomorrow?"

"Tomorrow's Sunday. I go to church in the morning."

"You don't go to church in the afternoon. Come on over, and we'll practice some more."

"Why don't you come to church with me? You'd all be welcome."

"Well, we're not much for church."

Dixie did not insist, but she said to herself, *One of these days I'm going to get every member of this family into church. Just see if I don't!*

When she got home, she found Ollie waiting for her. "Where have *you* been?" he complained.

"I was taking a riding lesson."

"Oh, for crying out loud. You can't spend all of your time with those gypsies!"

"They're Romanies, not gypsies!"

"Well, excuse me! I like them, but you can't spend your whole life with them!"

"Why are you mad, Ollie?"

"I'm not mad. I just think you need to pay attention to your friends. Like me."

Dixie stared at him. "Can't I be friends with you and Manny and Sonia at the same time?"

Ollie kicked at a clod of dirt. "I guess so."

"Look, the Romanos family needs all the friends they can get. They need you too, Ollie. I want you to be especially nice to them."

"I *am* nice!"

"But some of the kids aren't."

"Yeah, I know," Ollie said. "The guys listen to that knucklehead Billy Joe Satterfield."

"And the girls listen to Francine. They don't like anybody that's not just like them." Then Dixie said, "Let me fix an afternoon snack for Uncle Roy and Aunt Edith and start the washing. Then you and I can go fishing."

Ollie brightened at once. "That's great!"

"There's a good place over on the Romanos land. Maybe Manny can go with us."

Ollie's face fell, but he said, "The more the merrier, I always say."

"That's what I always say, too. Come on. You can help me fix sandwiches."

6
"A THIEF IS AMONG US!"

Ollie and Patty Peck were walking home after school when somebody called their names. They turned and saw Francine Mosely hurrying toward them.

"Wonder what she wants?" Ollie asked. He'd always thought Francine was stuck-up.

"I don't know, but you be nice!" Patty admonished him.

"I'm always nice."

"No, you're not."

Ollie had no chance to argue, for Francine came up.

"Guess what?" she said excitedly. "Daddy's going to take us all to Six Flags!"

"Oh, that'll be fun!" Patty exclaimed.

"And he's renting rooms for all of us so we can stay *two days.*"

"All who? And why's he doing this? It's not your birthday, is it?" Ollie asked.

"It's a reward for making good grades," Francine said smugly.

"Good grades? Why doesn't he give *me* a special reward? I got good grades!" Ollie bantered.

"Oh, hush, Ollie!" Patty said. "Let Francine tell about the trip."

"Well, we're going to get out of school Friday. We'll drive down to Six Flags and stay all night and all day Saturday."

"How are we going to get out of school?"

Francine shrugged. "Oh, Daddy will fix it with the teachers."

"Who's going?" Ollie asked suspiciously.

"You two, Billy Joe, Leslie and Kelly . . ."

"What about Dixie? She's going, isn't she?"

A scowl crossed Francine's face. She sniffed and ran a hand over her hair. "She's too busy reading palms with gypsies!"

Ollie frowned. "You ought to ask her," he said.

"It's my party, and I can ask anybody I want to! She's spending all her time with that gypsy trying to learn how to ride the barrels." Francine smiled then. "I hope she does enter the barrel-riding contest. She'll find it's not as easy as she thinks."

By the time Ollie and Patty reached the steps to their house, they were arguing.

Patty said, "It's her party, and she *can* ask anybody she wants."

"I don't care! It's not right!"

"Well, if you had a party, you wouldn't want to ask just anybody!"

"I'd want to ask my friends!"

"Hey, hey, what's the argument about?" Their father, Sheriff Peck, met them at the door. Usually he was at his office at this time. "It seems like you two spend an awful lot of time arguing. What's it about this time?"

"It's about that old Francine Mosely," Ollie said. "Her dad's taking her to Six Flags, and she's asking some of the kids to go along."

"Did she ask you?"

"Yes—but she didn't ask Dixie, and I don't think that's right."

Patty jumped into the conversation. "I was telling Ollie that it's Francine's party, and she can ask anybody she wants to."

"I reckon that's right," the sheriff said.

Ollie stood with his feet planted and a determined look on his face. "I don't care what anybody says! If she leaves one of us out, it's just because she's mean!"

Sheriff Peck looked down at his son. He was a big man, tall and with black hair. His boy looked like him. And maybe he was thinking Ollie had the same stubborn streak he had himself.

"Patty's right about this, Ollie. Francine can ask anybody she wants to."

Ollie argued some more until finally his father ended it.

"You'll just have to learn to live with what people do, Ollie. If you don't want to go, you don't have to."

"All right, I won't, then!"

"Oh, Ollie!" Patty said. "I don't want to go by myself. That old Billy Joe Satterfield always pinches me, and you have to protect me."

"Punch him," Ollie grunted. But then he said, "All right, I'll go. But I don't like it. It seems to me—"

Ollie never finished whatever it was he was going to say. A loud knock came at the front door.

"Who can that be at this hour?" his

father grumbled. He opened the door, and the sheriff's deputy, Seth Carmichael, was standing on the porch with another man.

"What's the matter, Seth?" the sheriff asked. "And what are you doing here, Nolan? Trouble?"

Nolan Fletcher was a little man who owned a farm just south of town. He was wearing a pair of faded overalls.

"It's one of my horses—that new gray mare I bought from Henry Thomason."

Sheriff Peck frowned. "Don't tell me she's lost," he said. "That's an expensive horse."

"You bet she's expensive. She's gone and I want her found!"

"He knows who done it, too!" Seth said. "It was that gypsy fella. That's who it was!"

Patty and Ollie moved in closer.

Sheriff Peck stared at his deputy, then turned back to Nolan Fletcher. "You saw him take the horse, did you, Nolan?"

"Of course I didn't actually see him." Fletcher shook his head. "What kind of a thief would that be?"

"How do you know he took her, then?"

"Because he's a horse thief, that's why!

Everybody knows that! He stole the Mosely girl's horse, didn't he?"

"No, he didn't!" Ollie interrupted loudly. "He found it and was bringing it back!"

Nolan sniffed. He turned to the sheriff. "You don't know these gypsies like I do, Peck! A bunch of them come through when we lived in Missouri. And when they left, they stole everything that wasn't tied down!"

"Well, you obviously don't like the Romanos family," Sheriff Peck said. "But I've got to have a little more proof than just your word."

"I followed their tracks, and they led straight toward the Romanos place!"

"Did you track the horse into their barn?"

"No, the rain washed out the prints, but they was headed straight that way, and that's why I come right to your office. Now, let's get out there! You'll find my horse in that barn, I promise you, Sheriff!"

Ollie's father heaved a sigh. "All right, we'll go out and take a look. You wait here, Nolan. I don't need you."

"Wait here?" Fletcher snorted. "Not likely! I want to be in on this!"

"Me too, Sheriff!" Seth said eagerly.

"You go back to the office and mind the store," Sheriff Peck told his deputy. "I can take care of this."

Ollie said, "Can I go with you, Dad?"

"No, we don't need you, either. I'll tell you all about it when I come back." Sheriff Peck took his hat off a peg and jammed it on his head. "I guess you can go along, Nolan. I think you're wrong, but it's my duty to check it out for you."

Dixie sat on a box outside the Romanos house, listening to Mr. Romanos play his violin and talk about the Romany people.

"Where do the gypsies come from, Mr. Romanos?"

He put the fiddle in his lap and smiled at her.

"Some of my people say we come from the Holy Land. Others say we come from Egypt." He laughed deep in his chest. "Some even say we built the pyramids. Other people say we come from Ethiopia."

Manny was sitting beside Dixie, his legs crossed. He tugged at the red handkerchief around his neck. "There was a man in Greece a long time ago—he saw some Romanies, and he said they were sorcerers."

"That's not true, is it?"

"Of course not," Mr. Romanos said. "People tell all kinds of stories about us. Romanies once lived all over Europe, especially in Hungary. There was once a king named Sigismund, who liked the Romanies very much. The Romany women told his fortune, the men played music for him, they all danced, and the king honored them. But we've had hard times too."

"Tell her about the hard times, Papa."

A cloud passed across his father's face. "During the rule of the dictator Hitler, ten percent of the Romany people was destroyed by the Nazis. My own father died at their hands . . ."

"Oh, I'm so sorry!"

"But let's not talk about that. Romanies like music. Why don't you sing a song for us, Dixie?"

"I don't know any gypsy tunes!"

"Then I will teach you one." He began to play again.

But Manny lifted his head. "Someone's coming," he said. "I hear a car."

Mr. Romanos put down his fiddle and stood up as a black car came up the road, trailing a cloud of dust.

Dixie stood. "That's Sheriff Peck's car." She noticed that everyone seemed tense. *They're afraid,* she thought. *If I'd had as much trouble as they've had, I'd be afraid, too.*

The car stopped. Sheriff Peck and a man in overalls got out.

Dixie recognized Nolan Fletcher. She saw that he had a hard look on his face, and she knew something was wrong.

"Hello, Mr. Romanos," Sheriff Peck said.

"Hello, Sheriff." But Manny's father was not smiling. He looked at the sheriff's companion.

"Got kind of a problem here, Mr. Romanos," Sheriff Peck said.

Dixie knew that Ollie's dad was a good sheriff. He knew how to handle problems and people. But what problem was he coming about?

The sheriff said, "There's a horse missing from Mr. Fletcher's place. We thought it might have wandered down your way."

"Wandered nothin'!" Fletcher exclaimed. "He was stole!" His face grew red, and he pulled his hat down firmly. "Don't just stand there, Sheriff. Arrest him!"

91

"Be quiet, Nolan," Sheriff Peck said. "Nothing's been proven here."

Dixie looked at Mrs. Romanos. Her face was tense with fear. The younger children looked frightened, too. Manny was scowling.

"We have no horse here. I am not a thief."

"Well, there's a thief among us!" Nolan Fletcher shouted. "Sheriff, I want you to look all over this farm!"

"I can't do that without a search warrant."

"Well, why didn't you get one before you came?"

"You do not need a search warrant," Mr. Romanos said quietly. "You may look anywhere you please."

"That's mighty nice of you, Mr. Romanos. It would clear this whole thing up in a hurry."

"He's probably got him in the barn," Nolan Fletcher said.

"Come. I will show you the barn."

They walked all over the farm. The search did not take long for there were very few places where a horse could be concealed. But Fletcher insisted on looking in every grove and every growth of brush.

Finally, he exclaimed, "He sold him! That's what he's done!"

"You know, Nolan, Mr. Romanos could sue you for character assassination. I think he'd win too. He'd have me for a witness."

"You'd testify for *him?* This gypsy against me?"

"So far, he's in the right, and you're in the wrong. All you know is that your horse is gone, and you don't know who took him."

"I know, all right," Fletcher said. "Take me back to town. I'm going to turn this over to the state troopers!"

"You do as you want to, sir, but I am not a thief." Victor Romanos spoke steadily.

"Let's go, Sheriff," Fletcher muttered and went to get in the car.

Sheriff Peck said, "I wouldn't worry too much about this, Mr. Romanos. You're in the clear. I'm sorry. He's a little excitable."

"Not your fault, Sheriff."

When the sheriff and Fletcher were gone, Dixie said, "That was just awful!"

Manny nodded. "It's happened before —and it'll probably happen again."

Dixie did not stay long after that, for she saw that Mr. and Mrs. Romanos and even the children were upset.

That evening, Ollie came over to tell her about the trip to Six Flags.

Dixie listened, then said, "I wouldn't want to go, anyway. I'd rather practice riding."

"I won't go if you don't, Dixie," he said loyally.

"You go ahead, Ollie. Francine has the right to ask anybody she pleases."

After Ollie left, Dixie sat on the front porch and thought about what had happened at the Romanos home. "It's not fair," she muttered. "They haven't done anything wrong. I wonder why people have to be so mean!"

7

LEFT OUT

". . . and this is Linda . . . and this is her little sister. Her name is Leila. She's only nine, but Linda is fifteen."

Dixie sat on a quilt under the chinaberry tree in the backyard, and Candy Sweet was squatting beside her. Spread all around her were Barbie dolls, and behind her lay a box full of doll clothes. Dixie picked up a Barbie with blonde hair and blue eyes. "Don't you think Linda's pretty?"

"I guess so." Candy studied the array of dolls, seemingly confused by the number of them. "You have names for all of them?"

"Oh, yes! You see, this is Zach." Picking up a male doll dressed in a tuxedo, she said, "Linda likes Zach, but Zach really likes Doris. This is Doris over here," Dixie added, picking up a dark-haired doll wearing a swimsuit.

Candy finally said his legs ached, and he sat down, crossing them. He was a huge man, strong and tanned by the sun and very slow-spoken. He thought over everything he said before speaking it. He knew every square inch of the farm and how to do almost anything.

Candy's mild blue eyes went from doll to doll. Then he picked up one and said, "Who is this one?"

"Oh, that's Angel. He likes Ashley, but Ashley likes Leonard."

"Which one is Leonard?"

Dixie picked up a red-haired doll. "This is Leonard. He likes Margo, but he sometimes does things together with Ashley, and Angel doesn't like that. So . . ."

"Don't see how you remember all their names."

"Well, *you* know the name of every cow on the place, and we've got more cows than I have dolls."

Candy sat listening as Dixie talked on and on. She did know every doll's name and had made up a history for each of them. As she spoke, she changed the clothes on one, her fingers flying.

Candy said, "I never did see any people that looked pretty like these dolls. Most folks have freckles or *something*."

"I guess that's right. They make them prettier than real people."

He smiled slyly. "When you decide to get married, you might not find anybody so good-looking as Angel there."

"That's not Angel, that's Leonard." Dixie thought for a moment. "I know these are just dolls made in a factory. They can make perfect dolls. But all real people have faults, so I won't ever find anybody absolutely perfect." She sighed.

Candy glanced at Dixie. "What's the matter? You don't feel good?"

"Oh, I feel all right," Dixie said. She was holding the doll called Doris and had been changing her clothes from an evening dress to a safari outfit. After a while she said, as if it didn't matter, "Maybe I'm a little bit lonesome. All the other kids went off to Six Flags."

"Why didn't you go?"

"I wasn't asked."

"Why didn't they ask you?"

Dixie wanted to blurt out all her troubles, but somehow she felt that wouldn't be right. She did say, "Well, it was Francine Mosely's party, and we've had a little argument, so she just didn't ask me."

"I reckon that hurts your feelings."

Dixie started to say no, but then realized that was not true. "Yes, it does, Candy. She's got lots of money and lots of nice clothes. And at school there's a group that hangs around her all the time. They do everything she says. They can be awfully cruel to people."

"Why do they want to do that?" Candy put down the Leonard doll, then set his straw hat on the grass beside him. "Why do they want to be mean?"

Dixie had thought about that herself. She said, "Everywhere I've ever been, it's been like that. A little group in school will get together, and they'll form sort of a club. Oh, they may not call it a club, but that's what they are. Everybody wants to be in their club, but they won't let them in. If they let everybody in, they wouldn't be exclusive, I guess."

"What's exclusive?"

"It means you keep everybody out except a few."

Candy picked a dandelion. He stared at it for a while, then blew on it and watched the tiny white particles float slowly to earth. "I ain't never belonged to no clubs myself."

Dixie suddenly felt sorry for the big man. "I'll tell you what, we'll form our own club. You and me, Candy. But it'll be different. We'll let anybody in that wants in."

"We won't be exclusive, then?"

"No. Anybody that wants to can join our club. We'll call it the Dixie and Candy Club."

He seemed to like that. Then he said, "There comes Manny on his bike."

"He looks mad."

"Sure does." Candy got to his feet. "Hi, Manny."

"Hello, Candy," Manny said shortly, laying down the bicycle.

"Me and Dixie just started a new club. It's the Dixie and Candy Club. But if you want in, we can call it the Dixie and Candy and Manny Club."

The simplicity of the big man drove away some of Manny's bad humor. He managed a smile. "Sure, I'd like to be a member. How much are the dues?"

"What are dues?" Candy asked.

"Some clubs make you pay to join."

Candy laughed. "No, this is free. Dixie, I'll go see if there's any of that banana cream pie left. If your uncle ain't et it all, we'll have Dixie Morris's banana cream pie."

"Sounds good," Manny said. He watched Candy start toward the house. Then he sat down beside Dixie. "He's a nice man. I wish everybody was as nice as he is."

"He's been my friend ever since I came here," Dixie said. "I didn't understand him at first, but he helped me take care of Jumbo when I found him in the woods."

Manny leaned on his elbow and picked up a dandelion. As Candy had done, he blew on it. Then he seemed to lose his good humor again. "I'm still mad about that Nolan Fletcher accusing us of stealing his horse."

"Oh, he's just an old grouch! You can't pay any attention to him."

"He wouldn't have accused you that way. Or anybody else. Only gypsies."

Dixie felt sorry for Manny. "I wish he hadn't done that, but it'll be all right. You want to play with my dolls?"

Manny stared as if she had asked him to jump over the barn. "Boys don't play with dolls."

"Some of them do. I had a friend in the circus, a real nice guy. He can make an elephant do anything, and *he* liked to play with dolls. We played all the time in our trailer. Then we'd play Monopoly."

"Well, I'll play Monopoly but not dolls."

Dixie laughed. "You're afraid somebody will call you a sissy!"

"They've called me everything else. Why should I care if they call me that?"

"All right, then. Show me you're not afraid to be called a sissy. I'll name all my dolls, and you see how many you can name back." It was a game that Dixie had played with her circus friends.

She was amazed when, after she'd named the dolls just once, Manny went around and named every one of them.

"Why, nobody's ever done that, Manny! You must be real smart."

He grinned briefly. "Anybody can name dolls." But then he said, "I'm ready to move on. I told Papa we ought to get out of here."

"Oh, no, Manny, you can't leave!"

"That's what Papa said. He said it'd be the same anywhere else we go."

Dixie studied the boy across from her. His black hair glistened in the sun as if it were wet. His handsome face was frowning. She said quickly, "I know what. Let me put these dolls away, and we'll go practice riding the barrels."

"You still going to go through with it?"

"Of course, I'm going to go through with it."

Manny raised his eyes. "People won't like it that you're friends with a gypsy."

"They don't like it, they can go sit on it!" Dixie said. "You and I are friends. Come on. We're going to practice."

Dixie packed away the dolls, with Manny helping rather awkwardly. She put them in the house, and then they biked down to the Romanos place.

When they reached the barn, Manny said, "I'm going to show you something else about horses today. I'm going to show you how to clean up after them."

"But I was going to practice riding."

"That's the fun part," Manny said, "but *some*body has to clean up after the horses."

Dixie soon discovered that horses made quite a mess, and she learned to do what Manny called "mucking out the stable." It simply meant cleaning it up—getting out the old straw and the mess the horses had made and putting in fresh straw.

When that was over, he showed her how to groom Champ with a brush. The horse liked that. He tossed his head and whickered.

"There, Champ, you look great!" Dixie said as she finished.

"You saddle and bridle him," Manny said. "It's time you did it by yourself."

Dixie looked at the muscular horse. "All right, I'll do it. All by myself."

She was pleased that Champ stood very still while she put on the blanket. She had practiced with the saddle and this time managed to throw it over, although the horse was much taller than she was. She tightened the cinch the way Manny had showed her. Finally, she slipped the bridle over his head. "Open your mouth, Champ." And when the horse did, she quickly fastened it.

"Look, I did it all by myself!" Dixie beamed.

"Good job. Now you've got to cut some seconds off your time."

For the next hour and a half Dixie practiced riding Champ. It was hot work, and she and the horse were both sweaty when they were through.

"Now you can walk him and cool him off," Manny said.

And holding the reins, she walked the horse back and forth, while Manny sat back against the barn, chewing on a straw and grinning and telling her stories of horses and things that she needed to know in order to be a good barrel rider.

After a while, he said, "I guess that's enough. We'll give him a feed now and go back to the house."

They watched Champ as he chomped some grain. Then Dixie rubbed his nose, saying, "Good-bye, Champ, I'll see you later."

On the way to the house, Manny said, "I hear the whole bunch went off to Six Flags without you."

"Oh, I didn't care about going, anyway."

"Didn't you?"

Dixie quickly looked at the boy. "Well, I did really, but there wasn't anything I could do about it."

"Did Francine leave you out because of me?"

"It wasn't just that, Manny. Let's not talk about it."

Later, Dixie pedaled slowly on her way home, looking at the fluffy clouds that crossed the sky. And then she said aloud, for there was nobody to hear her, "I don't know why people have to be like they are. Why can't they all just be nice to each other?"

Uncle Roy came out of the house and saw Candy cutting the grass in the front yard. "Candy, have you seen Dixie?"

"No, I ain't, Mr. Roy."

"See if you can find her. It's about time for her to get ready for that rodeo. I know she wouldn't want to miss that."

"OK. I'll see if I can find her."

Candy shut off the lawnmower and walked toward the red barn. He called Dixie's name and thought he heard a faint reply. "Where are you?"

The voice came louder. "Back here. Behind the barn."

Candy found Dixie seated against the back wall of the barn. She was wearing her rodeo outfit—a pair of tightfitting jeans, a colorful lime green Western shirt, and a cowboy hat just her size. She did not get up. She just looked at him.

"Your uncle says you better hurry. You're going to be late for the rodeo."

Dixie did not answer, and Candy saw that her hands were clasped so tightly together that her knuckles were white.

"What's the matter?" he asked. He squatted down, studying her face. "You look a little peaked."

"I'm all right."

"Are you sure? You don't need to ride no horse if you're feeling bad."

Dixie bit her lip. "Candy, I'm scared."

"You're scared you'll fall off and get hurt?" He was surprised. She had been telling him for weeks now that she had found riding a joy. "You never said nothing about that before."

"I'm not afraid of falling off Champ," Dixie said nervously. "I'm afraid I'll *lose.*"

Candy pulled off his straw hat and turned it around in his big rough hands. "Well, what's so bad about that? Somebody's got to lose."

"I know, but I feel like I'll be letting Manny and his family down if I lose. They've

110

had enough trouble with the people in this town without that."

"Maybe you won't lose," Candy said. "Maybe you'll win."

"I don't think I can," Dixie said. She got to her feet and brushed off the back of her jeans. "I'd like to just go in my room and shut the door and not come out."

"What would that help?" Candy asked. "I don't think you ought to worry about losing so much. Just do the best you can. That's all anybody can do. Even a mule."

"Oh, Candy, you just don't understand!"

Dixie had kept her feelings bottled up within her for a long time. Now she let them rush out. "You see, I've bragged in front of everybody how I was going to beat Francine Mosely, and everybody says Francine's got the best horse in the county, and she's been riding a long time, and she's had good teachers. And I haven't been riding but just a little while, and Champ's a good horse, but he'll be up against hard competition, and . . . what if I let him down?"

"Why, he won't know! He's just a horse!"

Dixie knew that this was true. In a barrel race, the horse being ridden never knew how well the others had done. It wasn't like a race where two or more horses lined up and each tried to be first.

"I'm just being silly. I know I'll have to go, but I'm so nervous. I'd hate to let the Romanos family down."

"You won't. I'll cheer for you."

"Are you going to the rodeo?"

Candy grinned and patted her on the shoulder. "You bet! I wouldn't miss it for anything. A member of the club is riding, ain't she?"

Dixie felt a little better. "All right," she said. "But you holler loud when I come into that arena."

"I'll do that," Candy said. "You ain't never heard how loud I can holler when I really want to."

"Let's go watch some of the events," Manny said to Dixie. "You won't ride for at least thirty minutes."

"All right," Dixie said meekly. She patted Champ on the nose, and he picked her hat off her head.

"Oh, give me that back! You're going to ruin it!"

"He likes your hat," Manny said. He stepped back and looked at her outfit. "You look real good, Dixie."

"I don't do too well in these high-heeled boots. I haven't learned to manage them yet."

"Well, you won't have any trouble when you're riding. As long as Champ's shoes are OK, you're OK."

They put the horse in a stall, patted him, and Dixie said, "We'll be right back, Champ."

Walking around the parking lot, Dixie saw that it was filled with mostly pickup trucks. "I never saw so many pickups in all my life."

"That's the kind of crowd you get at a rodeo. Even a high school rodeo."

The stands were crowded, but they finally found two places where they could watch.

Dixie said, "I'm so nervous, Manny, I don't think I can stay *on* Champ."

"Maybe I'd better get some duct tape and tape you to the saddle."

"Oh, be serious!"

"You'll be all right once you start. Everybody's a little nervous before their first ride. Look, they're going to have the bareback riding first."

The rodeo unfolded before them. It was about the same, Dixie thought, as a regular rodeo except that the contestants were all younger. All the bareback riders were boys, and Dixie yelled along with the others for her favorites.

"The next is the bull riding. I wouldn't get on one of those things for a million dollars!" Manny declared.

Dixie watched as a small Brahma bull charged out of the chute sideways and began to buck. The boy on him lost his hat in the first jump. Then the bull began a circular motion like a corkscrew, and Manny said, "Uh-oh, there he goes!"

The rider fell in the dirt, but at once a clown was there to attract the bull's attention. The bull followed the clown, who popped into a barrel, hollow on both ends. Snorting, the bull began to push the barrel around, and everyone laughed.

"Looks to me like the clown takes more chances than the rider," Dixie said.

"They got a hard job. Those bulls are nothing to fool with."

Dixie enjoyed the calf roping. She watched the first contestant throw his rope and catch the calf. His horse stopped at once and began backing up.

"See how that horse holds the calf down? That's what I want to train Champ to do. A horse that's a good roping horse is worth a lot of money."

The next event was the bulldogging. A yearling shot out, and a rider came right after him. The boy caught up with the animal, slipped off the horse, grabbed him by the horns, and wrestled him to the ground.

"That looks dangerous!" Dixie said.

"I guess it is," Manny said. "One time I saw a fellow miss, and a horn caught him in the head. Knocked him cold as a wedge."

Dixie shivered. "I don't think I'd want to try anything like that. I'll just stick to riding the barrels."

"Never saw anybody get hurt riding the barrels," Manny agreed. "We'd better go get ready. The barrels will be next."

They went back to Champ's stall, and Manny led the horse out. "How you feelin', boy?" he said, stroking Champ's silky nose.

He laughed when Champ pulled his cap off. "You have a taste for caps and hats! Give that back!" He pulled it on and announced, "I think you'll come in second."

At that moment Francine came by, leading her horse, Thunder. She stared at Dixie. "So you're going to go through with it."

"Of course, she's going to go through with it," Manny said. "You didn't think she'd back off, did you?"

Francine tossed her head. She was wearing a beautifully designed costume consisting of a riding skirt, a colorful blouse, and a neckerchief. "You're going to be sorry about this, Dixie. Nobody can learn to ride the barrels as quick as you have."

Dixie was too nervous to answer. She swallowed hard and watched as Francine swung into the saddle.

"Come on, Thunder," Francine said. "Let's go win first place."

"And now the first contestant, Miss Francine Mosely! Keep your eyes on this young lady. She's a winner!"

Dixie moved to where she could see the arena. Francine spoke to her horse, and then she shot forward. She went around the first barrel, leaning into the turn, and Thunder drove for the second. She circled the final two barrels perfectly and came back.

The announcer said, "That's a sixteen-second ride! Let's hear it for Miss Francine Mosely!"

The crowd applauded enthusiastically.

As Francine walked her horse out of the arena, she smiled down at Dixie. "Now, let's see you top that."

Manny whispered, "Don't pay any attention to her, Dixie. Do your job. Let Champ have his head. He knows how to do it. You're just a passenger."

"All right, but I'm scared spitless."

"It's OK to be scared. Just stay on."

There was one more contestant before Dixie's turn. The girl managed to knock over one barrel.

Manny said, "You're on next, Dixie."

"I just hope I don't make a mess of it."

"You won't."

And then it was time. Dixie kicked Champ into action. He shot forward as if she had touched a switch, and then she was out in the arena. She had never had so many people looking at her in all her life, but Dixie was not looking at the crowd. She saw one thing, and that was the barrel to her right.

"Come on, Champ, do it!" she cried. She could hear the tattoo of his hooves on the hard ground and was aware of the smell of dust. When they reached the barrel, she threw Champ slightly, but he knew what to do. She leaned into the turn to give him better balance and heard his hoofs scrabbling in the dust.

Then she kicked his sides, and they were off for the second barrel. "Come on, Champ!" she urged him. "We can do it!"

Champ approached the barrel, and then Dixie made the mistake of looking at the crowd. All those faces were looking right at her! She was so frightened by this that she did not know she had thrown Champ off stride. He rounded the barrel, but she pulled him too close, and the barrel went over.

Oh, no, I knocked over a barrel! There was nothing to do about it, though. Manny had told her over and over again, "If you knock over the first barrel, go to the second one. If you knock that over, go to the third. Do your best, no matter what happens."

Now, with his words ringing in her ears, Dixie drove for the third barrel. But it was even worse this time. She was so nervous that she jerked the reins. Champ's shoulder just touched the barrel, and it went rolling. Dixie felt tears come to her eyes.

"Well, that's tough luck for the young lady's first ride, but she'll do better next time! Let's hear a little applause for that rider!"

Dixie wanted simply to disappear from the face of the earth. She rode to where Manny was standing and fell off the horse.

He grabbed the reins, saying, "Don't worry about it, Dixie. It happens to everybody."

"I was just awful!"

"It's OK," he said. "There's always another rodeo."

"Well, I guess you see what it's like now."

Dixie looked around quickly to see a smiling Francine.

"Now, you don't have to bother with this anymore."

"Why don't you butt out, Francine?" Manny said.

"Why, you little creature! You're nothing but a horse thief! You ought to be in jail!"

Then Dixie flared up. "I don't want to talk to you, Francine!"

"I wouldn't think so, after the mess you made of that ride!" Francine snapped.

As the girl turned and walked away, Dixie began to cry.

"Here," Manny said awkwardly, offering his red handkerchief.

Dixie quickly wiped her eyes.

"Better blow your nose, too."

She did.

"And stick it in your pocket. But don't cry anymore."

"Everybody saw it—me knocking those barrels over, right and left." She leaned against Champ's side and said, "I'll bet you're ashamed of me, Champ."

Champ plucked off her hat. He tossed it up, then nipped at her hair.

"See, he's not mad at you. Nobody is, Dixie, except that Francine, and who cares what she thinks?"

"I can't do it anymore, Manny."

"Can't do what anymore?"

"I can't ride anymore."

"Sure you can," he said. "We'll practice some more. You'll be all right. The big Fourth of July rodeo is coming up in a month. We'll have plenty of time to practice, and we can go to a couple more rodeos and get you some experience."

Dixie looked at him. "I don't see why you're not mad at me."

Manny grinned, and his teeth were white against his olive skin. "Hey, you left one barrel standing. Next time you'll leave two, and then three. It's *OK*." He struck her lightly on the arm. "Losing's part of rodeoing. Everybody loses, even the best."

"Really?"

"Sure. Even the all-time rodeo champions don't win every time. Now let's go watch the rest of the rodeo. Then we'll go to Baskin Robbins. I've got enough money to buy you a banana split."

"OK, Manny." Dixie suddenly felt warm. "It's so nice to have a friend that doesn't get mad when you mess up."

"Well, it's all in our club." Manny smiled back. "Now let's watch somebody fall off a horse."

9

THE VISITORS

For several days after Dixie's disastrous ride, she was very quiet, both at home and at school. Part of this was due to Francine Mosely's insistence on relating the results of the race to everyone who would listen. She even managed to work it into the discussion in Mrs. McGeltner's English class.

Dixie made no attempt to defend herself. She was ashamed of the way she had bragged about winning. She made up her mind that she would never again, *ever,* brag about how she would do anything.

More and more, Dixie found herself drawn into the lives of the Romanos family. She grew very fond of Emily and Rolf. Sonia, the third grader, was thrilled when Dixie invited her to sleep over one night. It was the first time Sonia had ever done such a thing.

The next day was Saturday. After breakfast, Dixie took the little girl back home, and Sonia babbled like a magpie about the good time she'd had.

Mr. Romanos gave Dixie a pleased look. "I'm glad you and my children are such good friends, Dixie."

Dixie felt her face redden. "Oh, it was fun, Mr. Romanos!"

"Well, you must stay for lunch. Mrs. Romanos is going to make you a special rabbit stew."

Dixie called her aunt and uncle to tell them, and then Emily grabbed her by the skirt, saying, "Play!"

Dixie laughed, and they began to play the simple games that Emily liked so much, while Manny sat by and watched.

Finally freeing herself from the little girl, Dixie went with Manny and the other two children out to the pond. They fished for a couple of hours. The pond was full of plump sun perch, and by the time Mr. Romanos came to call them to eat, they had a stringerful.

"I like to catch fish, but I sure hate to clean them," Manny said.

"I'll help you after lunch. I don't mind."

"I never knew a girl that could clean fish. It's a messy job."

"So is cleaning up after a horse, but it has to be done."

When they were gathered around the table, Mrs. Romanos filled each plate with luscious, steaming stew. Then, coming back to take her own place, she said, "Dixie, eat up."

Dixie hesitated, then said, "Would it be all right if I said a thank-you prayer for the food?"

"Of course," Manny's father said. "Go right ahead."

Bowing her head, Dixie prayed, "Lord, we thank You for this food and for this time together. I thank You for the Romanos family and for the very special love we have for one another . . ."

When Dixie lifted her eyes, she found everybody staring at her. Even during the meal, she noticed that Manny kept watching her as if he had a question in his mind.

Dixie ate two bowls of stew, and then

Mrs. Romanos set out a fresh apple pie. As Dixie ate her piece, savoring the golden crust and the cinnamon taste, she said, "After church tomorrow, we're going to have a church picnic."

Manny raised his eyebrows. "You have a picnic in your *church*?"

Dixie laughed. "Not *in* the church! We go to church in the morning. Then, afterward, we go over to the park. Everybody brings something to eat, and we all share."

"That sounds like a Romany kind of thing," Mr. Romanos said.

"Oh, do your people like to have picnics?"

"We like to get together and sing and dance and eat. I suppose you might call it a picnic." Then he talked about the Romany people again. "We've always had rulers," he said after a while. "Even today, the head of a Romany tribe calls himself a king. Or if a woman happens to be the leader, she can call herself a queen."

"How many Romanies are there?"

"In this country? No one is sure. Probably over a hundred thousand. Twelve thousand live in New York City."

"Do they all live together?"

"Oh, no. Romanies are divided into a great number of 'tribes'— mostly English, Scottish, Hungarian, and Russian. And since each tribe has its own king or queen, there must be over a thousand Romany rulers in the world today."

"Maybe your family could all come to church tomorrow," Dixie said brightly. "And afterward we could all go to the picnic together."

The members of the Romanos family quickly looked at each other, and silence fell over the room.

"Did I say something wrong?" Dixie asked.

"No," Mrs. Romanos said. "You didn't say anything wrong, but I do not think it would be a wise idea."

"But we have a real good church. You'd like the preacher. His name is Reverend Stone. And you all sing so well—you'd pick up the songs we sing very quickly."

"I don't think I'd like to go." Manny shook his head. "We wouldn't be welcome."

"Of course, you'd be welcome," Dixie cried. But even as she spoke, she knew there might be a *few* who would not welcome the Romanos family. Unfortunately, there were a few old families in the church who didn't welcome *anybody* who hadn't been born within a mile of the church. Nevertheless, Dixie said earnestly, "I wish you'd all come. If you're going to live here, you need to meet people, and church is a good place to do it."

Mr. Romanos still looked uncertain.

And then Emily piped up. "Papa—picnic!"

Her father swept her up in his arms. "Picnic, is it? You always like a picnic."

Rolf and Sonia started in then, and finally Mrs. Romanos said, with some hesitation, "Maybe we *could* go, Papa."

"Please do," Dixie urged. "It will be such fun."

Victor Romanos, still holding little Emily, said at last, "I suppose we could, since you're so kind to invite us."

"Oh, good!" Dixie jumped up. "And bring your fiddle. Everyone will enjoy your playing."

Manny scowled. "I still don't think it's a good idea."

"Oh, be quiet, Manny!" Sonia said loudly. "Don't be such a sourpuss!"

"Who's a sourpuss?"

"You are!"

"Why don't I meet you all at the church?" Dixie said. "Be there at eleven o'clock."

"I will bring lots of food," Manny's mother said. "A special stew just for the picnic."

"Whatever you want to bring will be fine," Dixie said. "Some people just bring sandwiches."

But all the rest of the afternoon, Dixie wondered if she had done the right thing. It was not that she did not want the Romanies to come to church, but she feared that some people would not be friendly.

Lying in bed that night, she thought, *I'll just have to be extranice to all of them. And Reverend Stone—he always welcomes visitors.*

After breakfast the next morning, Dixie got into the truck with Uncle Roy and Aunt Edith. There was not room for Candy, so he sat in the back. He was wearing a pair of brand-new overalls.

Dixie had grinned at him, saying, "You're all dressed up for church."

"I sure like to go to church," Candy said. "I like the singing best of all."

"Don't tell Reverend Stone that. He'll get his feelings hurt."

Candy always took Dixie seriously. He nodded solemnly. "I won't tell him, but I do."

When they got out at church, Dixie said, "I'll wait outside so I can go in with Manny and his family."

"All right, dear. You want us to wait with you?"

"No, Aunt Edith. You go on in and find a good seat."

"I'll wait with you," Candy said.

It was a beautiful June morning. White clouds rolled across the sky, and the sun was not yet hot. The parking lot was nearly full, for most of the people had come earlier for Sunday school. But now other cars arrived, and those people who came for only the preaching service were filing in.

Dixie moved impatiently from one foot to the other. Then she straightened up and pointed. "Here they come, Candy!"

Up the road came the old pickup that Mr. Romanos drove. Mr. and Mrs. Romanos were in the front seat with Emily and Sonia. Rolf and Manny were seated in the truck bed with their backs against the cab.

Dixie ran over as soon as the truck stopped. "Hi! I'm glad you came!"

Manny jumped out and joined her. He looked worried. He said, "I'm not sure this is a good idea."

"Don't worry. You'll like church," Dixie said. "Hi, Rolf."

"Hi, Dixie. I have a new shirt!" Rolf was wearing a pair of light brown pants and a red-and-blue checkered shirt. He had an earring in his right ear, and then Dixie noticed that they all wore their earrings.

All wore colorful clothing too. Mr. Romanos had on a blouselike shirt with long, full sleeves. His wife had on a skirt and gaily colored blouse. Her black hair was neatly drawn back and tied.

Candy put out his hand. "Hello," he said. "Glad to see you this morning."

Mr. Romanos shook his hand and smiled. "Glad to be here."

Candy went around and shook hands with everyone, even little Emily. Her tiny hand was swallowed up in his.

She looked up at the big man. "What's your name?"

"Candy Sweet."

Rolf giggled. Maybe he thought the name was funny.

But Sonia whispered, "Hush, Rolf! You mustn't laugh at people's names."

"That's OK," Candy said. "People laugh at my name all the time."

Dixie led the way inside, and Candy brought up the rear. Mr. and Mrs. Romanos kept very close to each other, and Mrs. Romanos carried Emily.

There was a good crowd at church today. Most of the seats were already taken. Dixie looked around to find a place where they could all sit together but saw none.

The pastor was seated on the platform. When he saw them come in, he came down to meet them. "Well, Dixie, who are your guests?"

"These are my friends the Romanoses." Dixie introduced them one at a time, and Mr. Stone shook hands with each one.

"We're glad to have you. Let's see— you'll want to sit together." He looked over the congregation, then said, "Let me meddle a little."

A group of boys and girls were loosely scattered on one seat about ten rows from the front, and the pastor said, "Hey, kids, would you mind giving our guests this pew? I know you can find other seats with your friends."

One of the boys was Billy Joe Satterfield. He scowled and mumbled something to the boy next to him. But they all got up and moved.

"Thanks, kids," Mr. Stone said. "Well, here you go, folks. Nice seats close to the front. I hope you enjoy the service, and you'll be staying for the picnic afterwards, I hope."

"Thank you," Victor Romanos said. But he looked nervous.

Everyone watched the Romanies take their place in the pew. Their bright clothing made them stand out like exotic birds among a group of sparrows.

I wish people wouldn't stare so, Dixie thought. But then she shrugged, knowing that, whenever *any* strangers came in, they all had to endure stares. And the Romanoses *were* especially memorable.

The service started.

After the usual opening prayer and hymn, the pastor made the announcements. His last announcement was about the picnic.

"I would like to invite everyone to the picnic over at the city park after church. If you didn't bring any food, don't worry about it. We've got plenty for everybody." Then he said, "We have several visitors today. If you brought visitors, will you introduce them?"

Dixie waited until all the other visitors had been introduced, then she stood. "These are my friends the Romanoses. This is Mr. and Mrs. Romanos. This is Manny, Sonia, Rolf, and Emily."

"We're happy to have you, Mr. and Mrs. Romanos and all of you children. We'll expect to see you at the picnic."

From time to time during the preaching, Dixie stole a glance at her visitors. Emily was on her mother's lap the entire time. The other children sat as still as statues. The parents sat stiffly, too. She could not tell whether they liked the sermon or not.

The pastor preached on becoming a Christian. Then he said, "The Bible says whosoever will may come. We may be different in many ways, but at the foot of the cross, a king is no better than his poorest subject. The Savior died for all, and in the kingdom of God all are equal in need and are equally received. If you would like to trust in Jesus Christ, we invite you to come so that we might pray with you."

He talked about how to trust in the Lord Jesus. He quoted several Bible verses. One was: "The one who comes to me I will certainly not cast out."

The closing hymn began, and Dixie, sitting next to Manny, noticed that he seemed tense. "What's the matter?" she whispered.

"Nothing," he answered.

Still, his face looked strained, and Dixie wondered if he had had his feelings hurt somehow.

When the service ended, Pastor Stone said, "Now, we'll have our picnic. I challenge anyone here to a game of horseshoes, and the ladies will have the food set out very soon."

Dixie said, "I'll ride in the back of the truck with you and Rolf, Manny."

And then a terrible thing happened. Lester Mosely was standing at the church door. As the Romanos family approached, he said—in a loud whisper that could be heard by everybody for ten feet—"Ain't it a shame the kind of people that come into church wearing trashy clothes?"

Dixie wanted to fall through the floor. She knew that the Romanoses had all heard. She felt Manny stiffen. "Never mind him. He's that way with everybody," she whispered.

Lester was still staring at the Romany visitors. "Some people just can't stay with their own kind."

At that moment, Mr. Stone hurried forward. "That'll be enough, Lester."

Now Lester stared at the pastor. "Who do you think you're talking to? I'm a member of this church!"

"You may be a member, but I'm the pastor, and I'm asking you to leave before you insult our guests again."

Pastor Stone was a big man. Dixie knew he had been runner-up for all-American offensive guard during his college days. He still was strong-looking.

Lester mumbled, "We'll see about this later," and walked out.

"We certainly will," Mr. Stone said grimly. He turned to the Romanoses. "I'm so sorry. I wouldn't have had that happen for the world. Try to ignore him. I have to do it myself sometimes."

Mr. Romanos bowed his head slightly. "Of course," he said. "There are people like that among us as well."

"Well, I do hope you will come to the picnic."

"Yes, we're coming," Sonia said, "and you can have some of our rabbit stew, Reverend."

Pastor Stone laughed. "I'd like that. Nothing like good rabbit stew, I always say."

Dixie was still humiliated over the Lester Mosely episode. She went out quickly and got into the back of the pickup, sitting between Rolf and Manny. As soon as the truck started toward the park, she said, "I'm sorry about what that Lester Mosely said. Don't pay any attention to him."

Manny grinned suddenly. "I was going to kick him in the knee. That would have fixed him, wouldn't it?" Then he shrugged. "That's all right. I'm used to it."

"Well, you shouldn't have to put up with a thing like that in church."

The park was only a short distance from the church. Dixie saw that long tables were already set up, and it looked as if some of the women had missed the preaching in order to get the food ready.

Dixie introduced Mrs. Romanos to the pastor's wife and was relieved when Mrs. Stone said, "This stew looks delicious. Suppose we just put it right here where everyone can help themselves."

"It's only stew," Mrs. Romanos said apologetically, "but I used my own spices in it. Some I gathered from the field myself—like sage."

"It smells delicious, too," Mrs. Stone said. "I'd better get some before it's all gone."

The picnic dinner went very well indeed. The gypsy stew, once it was tasted, was gone almost at once, and so were Mrs. Romanos's pies.

The Romanies sat at one table, and the pastor and his wife sat with them. So did several other church members.

Afterwards there was a horseshoe tournament, and the pastor was amazed to find that he could not beat Victor Romanos.

"I was the champion around here until you came, sir," he said. "Now it looks like you're the champion."

"I've had lots of practice," Mr. Romanos said.

"Pastor Stone," Dixie announced, "Mr. Romanos brought his fiddle, too. He makes up songs himself."

"Is that right? We'll have a concert, then!"

The pastor got everyone's attention, and soon a large crowd had gathered around.

Victor Romanos went to the truck to get his fiddle, but he glanced around uneasily.

Mr. Stone cried, "Come on, Mr. Romanos, let's have a good tune! If you play something I know, I'll help you."

Mr. Romanos looked nervously at his wife, who nodded. Then he put the fiddle under his chin and drew the bow across the strings. The sound of sweet music filled the air. He played a hymn they had sung in church, "The Old Rugged Cross."

When he finished, there was enthusiastic applause.

Pastor Stone said, "You must have known that song."

"No, I never heard it before today."

"You mean," the pastor said, "that you

heard it just that one time and you could play it? That's marvelous!"

Sheriff Peck was standing close by. He said, "That's mighty good fiddle playing, Mr. Romanos. Could you play us a little gypsy music too?"

Victor nodded. "I will play you a song that has come down through the years. It is a song we Romanies play when we are happy."

It was a lively tune, indeed. Then he played several more songs before finally removing the fiddle from his chin and saying with a smile, "That is enough for me."

"We thank you for the concert," Pastor Stone said. "Well, folks, I've got to go and start reviewing my sermon for tonight." He turned back and shook hands with Victor, then with his wife, and then with all the children. "We've been so glad to have you."

"It's been a good thing to be here."

"We hope you'll come again."

Mr. Romanos looked at his wife, and when she smiled, he said, "Yes, we will come again."

Dixie walked with Manny back to the truck. She had not forgotten how nervous he had seemed in church, and she asked him about it. "Why were you so nervous during the invitation?"

"The invitation? What's that?"

"When Pastor Stone invited people to come forward and pray and trust in Jesus."

"I don't know. I just felt bad somehow."

"Maybe *you* need to become a Christian," Dixie said. "I did it three years ago."

Manny looked down at his feet, then muttered, "I don't know, Dixie—but I'll think about it."

10

MORE HORSE TROUBLE

I t seems we don't ever do anything but play with these dumb dolls!"

Patty Peck gave Dixie a surprised look. She had come for a sleepover, and the two girls, as usual, had spent most of the evening playing with Dixie's Barbie collection.

"Why, Dixie Morris, you love your Barbie dolls!"

"I'm getting too old to play with things like this."

"How old are you now, Grandma? Going on twelve?"

Dixie gave Patty a withering look. "I'm old enough to do things besides play with dolls." Suddenly she tossed her favorite Barbie across the room. As soon as she did, however, she went after the doll and began to smooth out its dress. "I didn't mean it," she said soothingly. Then she looked over at Patty. "I don't know what's the matter with me. I never do anything right anymore."

Patty was holding a Ken doll wearing a cowboy outfit. "*I* think you feel bad about not doing well at the last rodeo."

"I've ridden in *three* rodeos," Dixie said, "and I haven't even won third place!"

"You're getting better, though. The competition was pretty keen at all of them. You'll do better at the Fourth of July one."

Dixie shook her head. "I'm beginning to think you have to start this when you're one year old."

"Girls, it's bedtime!" The voice came from Aunt Edith and Uncle Roy's room.

Dixie said, "I guess we'd better go to bed. Tomorrow's Saturday, and I'm going to practice with Champ as hard as I can all day long."

The girls put away the dolls and climbed into the big double bed. As soon as Dixie turned out the light, it got quiet. But pretty soon she said, "I'm worried about Manny's family."

"Why?"

"It must be awful to go around with people suspecting you of being a thief. I don't see how Mr. Romanos stands it."

Patty said, "My dad doesn't think that he stole that horse."

"*He* may not think so, but other people do. That awful Lester Mosely is telling all kinds of stories."

"Well, there's nothing you can do about it tonight, so go to sleep."

Dixie knew that Patty was right. She was glad to hear that the sheriff did not believe Mr. Romanos was guilty, though. She prayed silently for the gypsy family, then finally drifted off and dreamed of riding Champ to victory at the biggest rodeo in the world.

"I'm going to fix the best breakfast you ever ate, Patty."

"I'll help. I'm not as good a cook as you are, though."

When they went downstairs, Uncle Roy was just going out the door to milk the cows. He stopped. "Did you girls sleep all right?"

"Fine, Uncle Roy. You hurry with the milking, now. We're going to have a great breakfast!"

Dixie had grown to love cooking. "We're going to have a big country breakfast," she told Patty. "How about eggs, and sausage, and grits, and homemade biscuits?"

"Can you make biscuits?"

"Sure I can. Uncle Roy won't eat the kind you make out of a box."

Soon she was introducing Patty to the art of biscuit making. Carefully she measured flour, baking powder, and the salt into a large bowl. She measured the shortening then and cut it into the dry ingredients. Then Dixie poured buttermilk into a measuring cup, dumped that into the bowl, and stirred until the mixture was moistened.

Patty sprinkled some flour onto the counter and scraped the biscuit mixture out of the bowl. Then Dixie kneaded the dough with a little flour, rolled it out, and cut it into round, thick biscuits.

When Uncle Roy came in bearing a pail of fresh milk, he sniffed, and his eyes lit up. "Candy's on his way. I hope you're making twice as much breakfast as we'll need. You know how much he eats."

When Candy arrived, he also sniffed the air. "That smells good," he said. "I gathered some eggs."

"That's another secret of good cooking, Patty," Dixie said, taking the bucket of eggs. "If you use fresh eggs, everything just tastes better."

When Aunt Edith came down, they all sat around the table. Uncle Roy started to bow his head, but then his eyes twinkled. "Do you girls want a long prayer or a short one?"

"A short one!" Dixie winked at Patty. "Sometimes Uncle Roy gets so carried away with his praying over the food that it all gets cold."

Uncle Roy, however, came through this time. He prayed a short prayer, then speared a biscuit with his fork and layered it with fresh butter. He rolled his eyes and said, "You make better biscuits than any-one—except for your Aunt Edith, of course. She's world-class."

Aunt Edith smiled. "I saw you wink at her! You really think she's a better cook than I am!"

"Well, you taught me, Aunt Edith. You and Aunt Sarah."

They lingered over breakfast, and just as they were ending the meal, Dixie heard a car pull up.

"That must be Daddy coming for me," Patty said.

Dixie went to the door and saw that it was the sheriff. "Hi, Sheriff Peck. Patty's about ready to go, but you better come in and have some of my good country breakfast."

Sheriff Peck came inside, but he shook his head at the invitation to eat. "I'm afraid I got some bad news," he said. "It's about Mr. Romanos."

Dixie's heart sank. "What's wrong?"

"It's Nolan Fletcher. He's brought charges against Mr. Romanos, and I've got to go arrest him."

Dixie stood still in shock. "That can't be true! He didn't steal that horse!"

"Fletcher says he's got a witness that says he saw the horse on the Romanos property."

"And I'll bet I know who that witness was!" Dixie cried. "It was that old Lester Mosely, wasn't it?"

"That's who it was, all right, but nothing I can do but arrest him."

"You mean he'll have to go to jail?"

"I'm afraid so, Dixie. For right now. I'm sorry. I don't want to do it, but a sheriff has to do a lot of things he doesn't want to do.

Come along, Patty. You can go with me."

"I'm going, too," Dixie said. "Will you take me over there, Uncle Roy?"

"Sure will." Uncle Roy got up, tossing his napkin on the table. Then he frowned at the sheriff. "Something's not right about this, Henry."

"I know it," Sheriff Peck said, "but, like I say, sheriffs have to do things they don't want to do. I doubt if he'll be able to make bail, either."

"What does that mean—make bail?" Dixie asked.

"It means that when somebody gets arrested, they can get out of jail until the trial if somebody puts up some money."

"I've got thirty-nine dollars in my savings bank," Dixie said. "Will that be enough?"

"I'm afraid not. Bail's always set at something like a thousand dollars."

"A thousand dollars!" she gasped. "Nobody's got that much money!"

Uncle Roy said abruptly, "Let's go see about it."

Sheriff Peck's office seemed crowded. Dixie stood to one side along with Patty, who edged in close to her. Sheriff Peck sat at his desk, and in front of him Victor Romanos slumped in a chair.

Mr. Romanos looked embarrassed. When his eyes met Dixie's, he muttered, "You don't think I did it, do you, Dixie?"

"Of course not, Mr. Romanos."

"He did it, all right!" Lester Mosely said. "I seen him leadin' that horse myself!"

"Put him in jail, Sheriff!" Nolan Fletcher said. "We're going to put a stop to all this stealing!"

"I been talking to the judge, Mr. Romanos. Your bail is set at two thousand dollars."

"Might as well be two million," Victor Romanos grunted.

Dixie felt like crying. "Uncle Roy," she said, "can't you do something?"

Her uncle had said little. But his usually mild brown eyes were sparkling. "I reckon I can. And I did. I already arranged for bail, so you just do your paperwork, Sheriff, so that Mr. Romanos can get out of here."

"You're going to let that varmint go loose?" Lester Mosely cried. "He'll steal another horse or something worse!"

"I reckon you can go now, Lester, and

you too, Mr. Fletcher," Sheriff Peck said firmly. "There'll be a hearing before the judge, but I don't need you here to do my job for me."

"You'll be sorry about this," Lester said viciously. He glared at Victor Romanos, then stalked out.

Mr. Romanos stood up and went over to Uncle Roy. "You're not going to put up two thousand dollars bail for me!"

"No," Uncle Roy said. "What we do is agree to pay ten percent of it. So actually it will be only two hundred dollars."

"I will work to pay you back, Mr. Snyder."

"We won't worry about that. What we got to do now is to prove that you didn't take that horse."

"I thought," Mr. Romanos said, "in America a man was innocent until he was proved guilty." He sighed heavily. "Here it seems, if anyone is accused, he is automatically guilty."

"Not that bad, Mr. Romanos," the sheriff said. "I don't think anybody would find you guilty on Lester Mosely's say-so."

"He's just trying to be mean," Dixie said angrily. "Don't worry. We'll find a way. We'll pray."

Mr. Romanos managed a smile. "You think God is interested in things like this?"

"Sure, He is," Dixie said firmly. "He knows when the sparrows fall." She looked over at Manny, who had accompanied his father, and as Mr. Romanos began to go over the paperwork with Sheriff Peck, she whispered, "Manny, don't worry about it. God will help us."

Manny had been silent all this time, but now he whispered, "Do you really think so?"

"Sure, I do! Let's just wait and see God rear back and do a miracle!"

11
THE DETECTIVES

The day after Mr. Romanos's arrest, Dixie could think of nothing else. She sat through her classes almost without hearing a word that was said.

One time Billy Joe Satterfield managed to make himself unpleasant by saying loudly in class, "I hear they finally got to the bottom of all this stealing around here. It looks like the gypsies have been doing it."

Manny, sitting next to Dixie, turned red.

Dixie grabbed his arm and whispered fiercely, "Don't pay any attention to him! You know he's always saying things like that."

During lunch hour, Dixie was pleased to see several boys and girls come by to say a word of encouragement to Manny. Ollie and Patty and Leslie and Kelly Stone sat at the table with them.

"We're all praying that God will help your dad," Ollie said. "He can do it, too."

Manny glanced at Ollie but said nothing. Dixie could tell that he was very discouraged.

Kelly glared across the room at Billy Joe Satterfield. "I'd like to drop him in a big hole somewhere!" he said.

"You're not supposed to talk that way about people," Leslie said. At twelve, she was one year older than her brother, and she tried to correct him whenever he stepped out of line. "You're not supposed to say bad things about people," she repeated.

"Well, what about *him?*" Then Kelly said, "Nobody likes Lester Mosely, either. He's the one that's caused all this trouble!"

"We all know that's true," Ollie said while eating his spaghetti. "I don't think he's got a single friend."

"And that's kind of sad," Dixie said.

Manny looked at her with a frown.

She said quickly, "I don't think he's right about your father, but I feel sorry for anybody that doesn't have any friends."

"He can have them if he wanted them," Ollie argued. "He's just ornery!"

As soon as the bell ended the last class, Dixie and Manny and their friends filed outside.

Leslie said, "We've got to pray for Manny's dad."

Dixie said, "We've already been doing that."

Patty leaned toward Manny. "It'll be all right. God can do great things."

At that moment an idea came to Dixie. She had been praying for God to show her if there was anything she could do. She was not sure this was an answer to her prayer, but she thought it might be. Excitedly she said, "I know what we have to do!"

"What?" Kelly asked. "You got an idea?"

"We've got to pray—but we've got to put *feet* on our prayers."

"What does that mean?"

"It means that, while we're praying, we've got to do everything we can."

Manny looked at Dixie, puzzled. "There's nothing to do."

"Yes, there is! We've got to become de-tectives. Somebody must have seen *some-*

thing of that horse. We know that your dad didn't take him, Manny, and we know that he didn't walk away by himself. So we've got to find somebody who *saw* something."

"That's an idea, all right," Ollie said. "Why don't we do it right now? It'd be better than doing homework."

"Anything's better than doing homework," Kelly agreed.

"What we'll do first," Dixie said, "is make a map. Then we'll go to all the farmhouses around your place, Manny, and we'll ask if anybody saw anything of that horse."

"Have you got a description of him?" Ollie said. "That's what detectives always say in books."

"Yes," Dixie said. "He's a big reddish-colored stallion."

"Must be a lot of those around," Kelly grumbled.

"Well, it's the best we can do. Let's go make the map."

The search took more time than Dixie had anticipated. It took all afternoon just to get the map made. But by Saturday they were ready to go. They all met at Uncle Roy's house at ten o'clock in the morning.

Dixie said, "We've got to be sure we go to the houses that aren't on the main road. That may be the very place where we find someone who saw that red horse."

She passed out the maps she had made, a separate one for each of the detectives. "Don't miss a house, and be sure that you get the time right when they saw the horse, and where they saw it, and who was with it. You got all that?"

"Sure. We can do it," Kelly said. "Let's go!"

They separated, and soon Dixie was pedaling her bicycle down a road north of the Romanos place. She stopped at the first house and balanced the bicycle against the white picket fence.

"Don't lean that bicycle on that fence! You'll spoil the paint!"

Dixie jumped, for the voice was loud. She turned quickly to see a large, heavyset woman coming around a corner of the house. She did not know the woman, although she thought she had seen her at Wal-Mart a few times.

"I'm sorry," Dixie said. "I didn't mean to do that." She quickly laid the bicycle down and then turned back to the woman.

But before she could speak, the woman beat her to it. "What do you want?"

"I'm trying to get some information—"

"You taking a poll or something? I don't have time for that! Off with you, now!"

"But, please, ma'am, I really need—"

"I'm busy, and I don't want any kids around here! Now get out!"

Dixie had to bite her lip to take the rebuke, but she saw there was no help here. She went back to the bicycle, picked it up, and pedaled off. She said under her breath, "I can't do this! It's awful!" Looking back over her shoulder, she saw the big woman staring after her as if she were a criminal.

"There must be another way. Everybody may act like that," she muttered. "We'll just have to think of something else." She thought about finding her friends and calling off the search.

But then she thought of Mr. Romanos and of Manny, and stubbornness rose in her. "I can't let some hurt feelings stop me," she said aloud. "We've got to find whoever it was who took that horse!"

* * *

"I don't think it's going to work, Dixie," Manny said wearily.

They were sitting on the porch of the Romanos house, and the family was gathered around. The sun was going down, and its red glow fell across the fields. It was a beautiful sunset, but Dixie could not enjoy it.

Still, she tried to be encouraging. "We just have to keep on going. We haven't been to half the houses around here."

"Whoever stole the horse must have been very clever," Mr. Romanos said.

She suspected he had little hope in what she and her friends were trying to do. "Mr. Romanos, did you know that even the heroes in the Bible had to go through hard things?"

Manny never read the Bible, Dixie had discovered. He said, "Just bad people should have hard times."

Dixie said. "There was a man called Jonah. He wouldn't obey God, and to get him to think and change his mind, God caused him to be swallowed up by a big fish."

"Well, that's a fine way to treat some-body!" Manny mumbled.

"That is the way I feel—that we've all been swallowed up by something," Mrs. Romanos said, but she tried to smile.

"While he was inside the fish," Dixie continued, "he realized that he had dis-pleased God. So he prayed, and God made the fish spit him out."

"What did he do then?" Sonia asked.

"He went and preached where God told him to, and a whole city was saved because he told them to turn to God and they did."

Everybody was quiet.

"And Jonah wasn't the only one," Dixie went on. "There was Daniel. He was a good man, but some people didn't like him, and they told the king lies about him, and the king put him into a den full of lions."

"Did they eat him up?" Rolf asked, his eyes big.

"No, God shut their mouths so they couldn't hurt him."

Mr. Romanos sighed deeply. "Well, we are not alone, it seems."

"No," Dixie said. "Everybody goes

through hard times. But God loves us. He wants us to know that."

"You really believe that?" Manny demanded.

"I sure do."

Manny suddenly grinned. "Well, maybe I'll just believe it, too! I'll trust God to get us out of the belly of the fish."

12

A SUGGESTION FROM CANDY

I'm starting to think it won't work, Candy," Dixie said sadly. She was walking along the path that led out to where the hogs were kept.

"What's not gonna work, Dixie?" Candy asked. In each hand he carried a bucket containing feed for the pigs. "You still worried about the Romanoses?"

"I thought sure we'd find *somebody* that had seen that big red stallion. But we must have gone to a hundred houses, and no one saw *anything*."

When they got to the pigpen, Candy put down the buckets and faced her. "How do you do it?" he asked.

"How do I do what?"

"How do you ask people?"

"Why, I just go up to the front door and

knock. And when they come, I ask them if they saw any big reddish stallion two weeks ago."

Candy thought that over. He chewed on a piece of straw. "Sometimes old people see things that younger people don't."

"What do you mean?"

"I mean—like *real* old people," Candy said. "Most people who aren't old have to work real hard. They don't have a lot of time for looking."

"What are you getting at, Candy?"

"I mean—maybe you're asking the wrong people. You know how Mrs. Simms down the road sits on her porch all day when the weather is nice. She sees everybody that passes down that road, I bet you."

Dixie looked at him, thinking. "You know, that's right! And I'll tell you someone else who knows about everything—little kids!"

"Yup. Kids see a lot," Candy agreed. "Maybe you'd better go ask some of them."

"That's what I'll do! I hope we haven't missed something along the way. I never thought of especially asking older people or children!"

Once the plan was in her mind, Dixie went into action. She studied her map, then got on her bicycle.

She pedaled directly to the road that lay beyond the Romanos house, then turned off onto a narrower road. This one had been a logging trail and was filled with deep ruts. But she could tell that cars or trucks came in and out occasionally. Avoiding the ruts, she kept going.

After a while, a rundown log cabin came in sight. At first she thought it was vacant. Then she heard voices.

Somebody lives here, she thought. She got off her bicycle and pushed it along. As she came into the clearing, three children came out, none older than six or seven. Their clothes were not very clean, nor were they. They stopped abruptly when they saw Dixie.

"Hello," she said. "How are you kids today?" She got no answer. Reaching into her pocket, she pulled out a bag of peppermints. "You want some candy?"

They came toward her then and held out their hands. They popped the candy into their mouths, and Dixie managed to get a conversation going.

"I bet you kids see everything that goes on around here, don't you?"

The biggest, a boy, said, "Guess we do. Can I have another candy?"

"Sure." Dixie handed out three more pieces and saw that they were not going to be saved for a later day. Knowing that her supply was small, she quickly began to ask questions. "Have you seen a big red horse?"

"You mean today?" The smallest of the group, a dark-haired girl, stared at her with big eyes. "We ain't seen no red horse today."

"No, it wasn't today," Dixie said. "It was a while ago. About two weeks ago." She watched their faces.

The oldest said, "Yeah, we seen a big red horse."

"Are you sure it was red?"

"Sure, it was red," the older boy snorted. Then he asked, "Can I have another candy?"

Dixie felt this was worth the investment. She held up the sack and said, "If you can tell me about that big red horse, I'll give you the whole bag."

"I'll tell!" the middle child said. She

pointed to the road. "It was almost dark, and this man he come past leading that big red horse."

"Where does that road go?"

"It winds around for a spell," the older boy said. "Then it comes out at a farm-house."

Dixie questioned them at length, but they could tell her no more.

Finally she said, "Thanks a lot." She gave them the rest of the candy and picked up her bicycle.

It was getting late in the afternoon, and she did not know what lay ahead, but she thought, *I've got to find out something, and this is the first lead I've had.* She continued down the road.

For fifteen minutes or so, Dixie pedaled along the trail. And then she heard a dog barking. She stopped and concealed her bicycle in the bushes, then crept along quietly until she came to the edge of a clearing. In the clearing was a corral. And in the corral stood a big red horse!

"I found him!" Dixie whispered. Then the dog barked again, and it seemed closer this time. *I'd better get out of here,* she thought. *I've got to get back to town.*

When she reached the bicycle, she turned it around and began pedaling as hard as she could. But she remembered to say, "Thank You, Lord, for helping me find the horse."

It did not occur to Dixie just then that it might be the wrong horse. She pumped until her legs grew weary. But she was happy because, she was sure, she had found the answer.

Sheriff Peck stared down at Dixie and listened as she excitedly told her story about finding the red horse. She was almost out of breath, for she had ridden her bicycle all the way to his office in Milo.

Then he made her go back and tell it again. Finally he nodded and said, "OK, let's go take a look." He lifted her bicycle into the back of his pickup. "You get in front, Dixie." He got in after her, started the engine, and they started back toward the farmhouse and the corral.

They passed Uncle Roy's house. Now that all this was actually happening, Dixie felt apprehensive, wondering if she had done the right thing.

As they passed the Romanos place, she

saw Manny out walking Champ. She waved at him. "Can't we stop and tell them what's happening?"

"Better not. It may be a different red horse. No sense getting their hopes up," Sheriff Peck replied.

Dixie nodded and then directed him down the little crooked road. "There's where I saw the kids who saw the red horse."

"May have to have 'em for witnesses. Hang on. This looks like a rough road. It's on down this one here?"

"That's right."

After a while Dixie said, "We're getting close now. If they hear a truck coming, they might take the horse away. You think maybe we ought to get out and walk?"

"That's not a bad idea. And it's what I was planning to do." He grinned as he pulled the truck to the side of the rutted road. "You'd make a pretty good sheriff."

They got out and walked. And when they rounded a bend, Dixie said, "There he is, Sheriff Peck! There's the horse!"

"That's the one, all right. I've got a good description of him. I don't think there could be two like that." He looked down at

Dixie. "Do you know whose place this is, Dixie?"

"No."

"It belongs to Lester Mosely. It's an old hunting camp. I've been here myself during deer season."

Dixie looked up at the sheriff and tried to understand what he was thinking. "Do you think *he* took the horse?"

"We don't know, Dixie, but I'm thinking nobody else comes back here." He looked over at the house. A thin line of smoke was rising from the chimney. "Somebody's here. We'll go find out. I think Mr. Lester Mosely has some questions to answer."

"You can let me out here, Sheriff."

Sheriff Peck looked over at the Romanos house and grinned. "I guess you want to give them the good news."

"I tell you I didn't steal that horse!" Lester Mosely was wedged between the sheriff and Dixie. He had a frightened look on his face. "He just wandered in there. I *found* him in my corral."

"I hope you got a better story than that for the judge, Lester. No horse could jump into that corral, and you know it. I think you're in big trouble this time—and I don't think your brother can get you out of it like he has before."

Sheriff Peck stopped the truck, and Dixie got out and shut the door.

The sheriff got out, too, and took down her bike. He smiled and said, "You're a good detective, Dixie." Then he looked over at Victor Romanos and his family, who were approaching. "I don't think you have to worry about anything, Mr. Romanos," he called. "Dixie will tell you all about it." He got in, stepped on the gas, and the pickup roared off.

The Romanos family gathered around. "What does he mean, Dixie?" Mrs. Romanos asked. She was holding Emily in her arms.

"It means that Lester Mosely took that horse."

"You found it?"

"It's a long story."

"Then you'd better come in and have something to eat," Victor Romanos said. "We want to hear all about it."

Dixie went inside with them and soon was into her story.

After the Romanos family had all listened with amazement, Manny finally summed it all up. "Wow, Dixie. God did get us out of the fish's belly, didn't He?"

"I told you He could." She smiled. "He wants people to know He cares about us."

"What will happen to Lester?" Mr. Romanos asked.

"The sheriff said he's in big trouble this time. Lester said he found the horse in a corral that no horse could jump. Sheriff Peck told me he thinks he just took the horse to make it look like you did it, Mr. Romanos."

"His brother's a rich man. He'll get him out of it," Manny said.

"Not this time. Sheriff Peck told me George Mosely was tired of Lester's doings. And besides, the sheriff's going to press charges."

"Well," Manny said, "maybe this story is going to have a happy ending after all."

Dixie felt so relieved that she laughed aloud. The Romanos family was going to be all right. And they were learning that God truly cared about them. Then she thought of something else. "One more thing will make it have even a happier ending."

"What's that?"

"When we win the barrel race and you sell Champ for a lot of money!"

"You know, I think it's going to happen," Manny said. He grinned at Dixie and looked around at his family. "She'd make a pretty good Romany herself, don't you think?"

13

PARTY TIME

Dixie sat tensely in the saddle, waiting for her signal to enter the arena. She reached down and stroked Champ's smooth hide. "We're going to win this time, Champ!"

She thought about how things had all worked out. Lester Mosely had been found guilty and had been sentenced to a year in jail. The sentence was suspended, but he'd been placed on strict probation. George Mosely told Mr. Romanos he was ashamed that a member of his family had done such a thing, and the Romany had accepted his apology in a graceful fashion.

A voice beside her said abruptly, "Go for it, Dixie!"

Dixie looked down at Manny. He was grinning, and he winked at her as if he hadn't a care in the world. "You can do it. I know you can!"

Suddenly, all her nervousness left. She grinned back at him and said, "All right. Here we go!"

She kicked Champ's sides, and he shot forward as if propelled from a gun. She heard her name booming over the speakers, but this time she blocked from her mind everything except the ride. As she entered the lighted arena, she could see only the first barrel.

She knew that she had gotten a good start. Leaning forward in the saddle, Dixie urged the horse ahead. "Go, Champ, go!"

She reached the first barrel and guided Champ closer to it than she had ever dared before.

The horse rounded barrel number one, dust flying. He was leaning over so far that Dixie had to hang on. As soon as he started scrambling for the second barrel, Dixie leaned forward even more. She knew that this was her big chance.

Champ rounded barrel number two and started for the final one. Dixie could hear the crowd screaming, but she never took her eyes off that third barrel. The muscles of the powerful horse moved beneath her, and when he leaned into the turn, she leaned with him to give him better balance.

She was still leaning to the side when he came out of the turn. "Go, Champ, go home!" she cried, and the quarter horse broke for the finish line. Dixie heard his hooves pounding. She heard the roar of the crowd. And then she swept into the shadow of the stands.

Dixie pulled Champ to a halt where Manny waited, and she all but fell out of the saddle. As she let go the reins, she heard the announcer say, "And it's fifteen and a half seconds for Dixie Morris! A fine ride for the little lady!"

"You did it, Dixie!" Manny shouted.

And Dixie thought she had never been happier in her whole life. As she and Manny hugged each other and did a victory dance, Dixie saw a crowd coming. It was Uncle Roy and Aunt Edith, all of the Romanos family, and what looked like ten or fifteen of her school friends.

And then she found herself patted and punched, while somebody shouted, "You won, Dixie! You won! Fastest time ever for your class!"

When her uncle and aunt hugged her, Dixie looked up at them and said, "I wish Mom and Dad could have been here to see that."

Uncle Roy's face broke into a broad grin. "They *will* see it. We got it all on video-tape."

The pool area was crowded. Mr. and Mrs. Mosely had told Dixie that she could invite anyone she wanted for a victory cele-bration, and she had invited fifteen or so classmates. Some of them had never been at the Mosely house before.

The celebration was an especially sweet victory for Dixie, for Francine had issued the invitation. Although Dixie knew that Francine's parents had pressured her into doing so, she had enjoyed hearing Francine say, "Dixie—well—you're invited to come to a party at our house."

"Oh, really, Francine! How nice of you!"

Francine had swallowed hard, but she'd managed a smile.

Dixie and Manny had both come dressed

in the best they had. Later there was to be swimming, but for now there were just snacks.

Manny looked at Francine, standing beside the pool with Billy Joe, and he grinned. "It sure bothers her to have a bunch like us here, doesn't it?"

"I think Francine's not as bad as she seems," Dixie said.

"No, she's not," Manny said. "She's worse." He grinned again. "I'm just kidding. I don't think she is, either. She couldn't be."

"You're awful, Manny!"

"I know. Let's go over and offer to let 'em go fishing with us."

Dixie giggled. "I'd like to see Francine put a worm on a hook."

They wandered over to the pool, and Dixie said as nicely as she could, "It's a fine party, Francine."

"Thanks," Francine said. She was wearing a new pink dress, and her hair had a new permanent in it. Dixie knew she had gone to the beauty shop the day before.

"How about if we all get some of those refreshments?" Manny said. "That cake looks pretty good."

Billy Joe Satterfield didn't seem fully ready to become a full-time friend of Manny Romanos. Nevertheless, he grunted, "OK by me."

Then, somehow—perhaps because of her high-heeled shoes—as Francine turned, her foot twisted. She made a wild grab for anything to help keep her balance and managed to clutch Billy Joe's shirt.

"Hey!" he yelled, but it was too late. Totally off balance, Francine fell toward the pool, dragging Billy with her.

Dixie made a futile try to help, but her fingers merely brushed Francine's skirt.

Francine screamed wildly. Billy yelled at the top of his lungs. It did not help. They both hit the water with a mighty splash.

Francine struggled to the edge of the pool. She spit out water and tried to wipe her eyes. Her hairdo was destroyed.

Dixie truly felt sorry for her. "Are you all right, Francine?"

"My hair—it's ruined!"

Manny wasn't polite. He laughed out loud. "Too bad, Francine."

Dixie didn't laugh, though. Francine had behaved badly. Still, the girl must feel awful. Suddenly, Dixie grabbed Manny by the arm and leaped into the pool, pulling him in with her.

"Hey, what are you—" when he came up, Manny finished his sentence "—doing?"

Dixie looked up at the other guests gathering around the pool. By this time, everybody was laughing. She held onto the side of the pool next to Francine and laughed, too. "It's a nice party, Francine!"

At that, Patty Peck and Ollie jumped in, followed by Leslie and Kelly Stone. And then everybody else was leaping into the water. There was not a single dry boy or girl at the party. They swam around in their clothes, and somehow it was fun.

Francine paddled close to Dixie and murmured, "That was nice of you, Dixie. I've been pretty rotten, and I'm sorry."

Dixie grinned. "That's OK. I always like to go swimming fully dressed."

She swam to where Manny was splashing water on Leslie Stone, and she pushed him under. That started a splashing party that lasted for the next ten minutes.

Then somebody yelled, "All right, all you guys, let's go for the refreshments!"

Dixie, not to be outdone, cried, "All right, girls! We'll go, too!"

***

From their living-room window, George and Mrs. Mosely looked out at the laughing, sopping-wet young people.

"That's terrible!" she said. "They're going to make an awful mess!"

George Mosely said, "Let them alone. Francine needs something like this. She's kind of stuck-up, you know."

His wife glared at him. "She is not!"

"Sure she is. It's hard to be stuck-up when you're soaking wet, though."

Outside, the guests gathered around the refreshment table and dug into the ice cream and cake.

Manny wandered over to Dixie. His clothes were wet. His black hair was matted. But he seemed happy. He whispered, "Congratulations, champ."

Dixie grinned at him. Her hair was plastered against her face and her clothes against her body, but she was happy, too.

"I wish Champ was here. I bet he'd like to swim in the pool."

"I don't think the Moselys would like that. And it wouldn't be good for him."

"As soon as we get away from the party, let's go to your house and practice riding some more. I believe I can cut a second off my time with some more practice."

"That's sure OK with me."

They turned back to the refreshments, each seeing who could put down the most ice cream, and Dixie Morris was happy indeed.

Moody Press, a ministry of the Moody Bible Institute, is designed for education, evangelization, and edification. If we may assist you in knowing more about Christ and the Christian life, please write us without obligation: Moody Press, c/o MLM, Chicago, Illinois 60610.